SHONASIA & X

A Miami Love Takeover

TISHA ANDREWS

Email: AuthortAndrews@gmail.com

Facebook: Author Tisha "Lil Drew" Andrews

Twitter: @tisha_p12

Instagram: @lil_tdrew and @lil_t_drew

Cover design: Briann Danae

❀ Created with Vellum

SYNOPSIS

Shonasia "Shona" Bradley hates love and anything that's affiliated with it. After years of loving an emotionally, unavailable man from her past, she's over it. Gone are the days of wishing she was wife and mother material while she throws herself into her work.

Unfortunately, the work she used to do in the streets seems to find her no matter how hard she tries to leave it behind.

Xander "X" West, a high-profile defense attorney, is over love, too. After what he deemed a perfect love affair that had gone wrong, he wants nothing to do with the likes of a woman if it goes beyond the bedroom.

That is until he meets Shona. Maybe, just maybe they are the cure for each other, but only trying love out will be the only way to tell.

Detective Ace Alexander, X's best friend, is wild and crazy. While fighting crime, he has no time for winding down with a lady friend or two. He's not fighting love, but he isn't looking for it either.

Gabriela Wilcox is not only brains, but beauty, who is stuck in a verbally and physically abusive relationship with her fiancé, Tyson. Tyson, to many, is a community role model, but behind closed doors, he's Gabriela's worst nightmare. The only way out for her it seems is death, until she meets Ace, possibly seeing another way out.

Find out how love can takeover a broken heart when there's nothing else left to give.

Note that this is a re-release.

This is a re-release as it was published under my former publishing company, Royalty Publishing House.

This storyline is a spinoff, picking up from *His Sky, Her Shyne: A New York Takeover*. In that series, Chico is found in the company of Shonasia "Shona" Bradley, his former ride or die chick although still very much married to his wife, Myriah.

Shona finally gets her own story outside of The Crew originally introduced in my breakout series, *The One that Got Away: A Miami Love Affair*.

You don't have to read those series to connect with Shona's story but I certainly won't stop you. I've seen growth in my storytelling but all of those characters are a part of me. So is Shona. Love her because I do. Be patient with her because I am. Take this journey with her as I give her a happy ending or not. LOL. But one never knows. It's all in how the characters choose to speak to me.

Thank you for supporting me as I go on this self-publishing journey! Oh, and if you haven't, go check out *When it Snows in Miami for Christmas*. There's more of The Crew in there.

<hr>

CHAPTER ONE

<hr>

September 2017

"It's that easy, Shonasia?" her ex Chico growled lowly, quickly pinning her against the wall. He was fast, snatching both of her hands by the wrists over her head. He lodged his knee between her thighs, the warmth between her legs welcoming him as he unbuttoned her trench coat. "Just like that? You leave and say fuck me?"

She shuddered, hearing the pain in his voice. It matched the one drumming in her heart. She tried ignoring it, but he wasn't playing fair. The raspy texture shook her soul, tearing down her resolve. He dragged his tongue up her neck. Her body stiffened while his tongue ignored the subtle rejection. He slowly sucked and pulled on her earlobe, driving her insane. It was then that Chico knew he had her.

"Ugh," Shona groaned, feeling him brick up pistol hard. The softness of her skin under his tongue drove him wild. She had him, too, as the tables turned in her favor. She knew it as he moaned. He only moaned in the past, times when he was most vulnerable. He could taste the Shea butter scrub coating his tongue. She squirmed, trying to loosen his grip, but couldn't.

"Para," he chided in Spanish, telling her to stop as he quickly looked both ways down the dark alley. She trembled, feeling the breezy

New York wind. "Baby, please," he whispered as his hardened member fought to get out.

He quickly released himself, dropping his sweatpants down just enough. He laid his forehead against hers, stroking himself. He wasn't thinking clearly, but she did that to him. She knew she could and now here she was trying to leave without as much as saying goodbye.

"Chico," she cried out, feeling her own center ache. "N—no. We can't."

"Mmhmm," he answered, her cry a delight to his ears. He couldn't take much more, sliding his callous fingers down into her leggings, cupping her sex. He dipped one finger in in, feeling the slickness pool down into his hand.

"Uh," she uttered.

"Shonasia, you're so wet for me. Why you playing?" he asked, the husk in his voice evoking more emotion.

She wiggled some more, her sex hungrily sucking in another finger. He pulled them out and stuck them in her mouth. She hummed and sucked so hard, he got jealous of his own fingers, snatching them out. He took her mouth and kissed her, chasing what was left. "Fuck. You're still so got damn sweet."

"Shut up," she hissed, mad she had given in to him.

Wasting no time, he pulled her leggings down, stepping on the crotch area until he freed one of her ankles. She cursed him until her words got lost once her second set of lips parted, granting him access.

"Shit," he growled, her pussy not easily giving in to him. He knew what an untouched vagina felt like, even the reformed virgins. He could tell she wasn't giving it up as it clamped on hard to his dick.

He smiled, watching her wince as he worked his way inside. He tucked his lips, biting down hard so he wouldn't sound like a bitch. It was something about deflowering a pussy, but just not any pussy. The pussy a man knew no one else had touched. He tongue-stroked her mouth while her center released a heavy shower of her essence.

If he wasn't in love, he sure felt like it now. Everything about Shona made him feel alive. She wasn't his wife, but she was once his best friend, his rider, and he wanted her more than he wanted to breathe, suffocating in her presence.

He smiled in her mouth, his strokes steady and slow. She was a product of him, teaching her everything from cooking dope to fucking as baby girl gave it up right outside. It was New York, a dirty alley at that, and she still gave in to him. Giving in wasn't something he got anymore at home, missing the submission of a woman.

"Tight lil' pussy ass," he muttered, trying to savor how pleasurable her walls were that clung to him.

"I told you to shut up," she fussed, working her hips.

Her mouth may have been saying no, but her body was riding him like a jockey does a horse. It was like old times. She was just sixteen and he was barely a grown man that somehow grew an empire that fed many. She was his trap queen, his bitch. No other could come close to claiming him, except one. That one he eventually married and had two children with. Her name was Myriah.

Myriah was no saint herself, the neighborhood promiscuous beauty queen that was like forbidden fruit. Sadly, by the time Chico fell in love with her, he learned she was already linked to his boy, his best friend. Behind the scenes, he had his way with her, while Shona rode shotgun in the daylight by his side. In this moment, he didn't know what his heart wanted but his dick was feigning for Shona.

"What, you mad?" he asked, chuckling as she frowned. "I don't know why when you're fucking me back, old mean ass girl."

"Ugh, move. Stop. Just stop," she whined, locking her legs.

"Oh, that's what we doing?" he asked her with a raised brow, standing up in the pussy. She gasped, feeling the head touch the tip of her heart. She gasped once more as he grinned and pushed up just a little. "We can do this all day, ma. All day." He bit her neck and she screamed as he covered her mouth with his.

"Mmmm, please," she tried to get out, as he kissed her neck.

"Calm your little ass down, Shonasia," he gritted, easing in and out of her more forcefully as her mouth fell open once he removed his hand. "You're finally getting this grown man dick again. This my pussy?"

"Fuck you, you little ass boy," she snarled, feeling her insides stretch even more for him. Still, she kept fucking him back, unable to deny him. "Never thought I would see the day you gotta take the pussy," she snarled, taunting him.

"This little boy fucking *his* little pussy though," he shot back.

Shona jerked her hips to the left and right, trying to get him to dislodge but he stayed with it, her juices wetting up the both of them. He looked down and his dick got even harder, her body greedily taking him in. "Look at it," he whispered. "Look at what you're doing to me."

She did and damn near stopped breathing. She stared in awe, watching this thick, pretty, brown muscle dance inside of her. He heard her coo as she bit her own lip now.

"Hot pussy self. Always acting like the victim," he teased. She snapped then, cursing him out. She even laughed and told him his stroke was weak and tired, but she still kept tossing him that wet pussy.

Then he stopped and pulled out, his body still pressed against her. His hot mouth found her neck and worked its way back up to her ear. She growled, feeling the cool air riding up her ass. Her lower lips ached, wanting him back inside of her.

"Naw, no more dick for you until you tell me that you're sorry." Her eyes bucked, praying he wasn't serious, but he didn't budge.

"Chico?" she whined, her voice quivering.

"Naw, ma. Say sorry." He smiled watching her squirm as he stroked himself against the outside of her sex.

She surprised him, hoisting her hips up and sliding back down on it with no hands.

"Oh, fuck," he hissed, ready to propose to the pussy as it sucked him in.

"Un huh," she said and smirked, watching him go from confused to excited. She slowly winded her hips, picking up the pace until she felt his balls tapping the bottom of her ass.

Not wanting to be outdone, he took control holding her hips. She started shaking while he bounced her up and down, showing her no mercy. She started to scream, her body coming apart until he felt a strong squeeze and a wetness escaping her body. "Ahhhh!"

"Damn! You've never done that for daddy," he said in amazement, leaning back to watch. He rubbed his thumb in a circular fashion, demanding she release more. And just like that, she went from begging him to stop to demanding he keep going.

Her voice clipped in the air, resorting to small whimpers. He then showered her face with kisses before his thick, wet lips landed on hers. "Bitch, I woulda killed you if you left without blessing me with this pussy," he mumbled, pumping hard as he tried to punish her. He was angry again and she knew it.

"What?" she spat, snapping out of it as her own rage unleashed. Just like that, she felt stupid, remembering how she felt played just a few hours earlier. They hadn't seen each other in years. She was only in New York for business, but him being there made it personal.

Soon, he led them down memory lane and she followed. They were ending the night as two old friends, former lovers finding closure, or so she hoped by staying in touch. That was until he reminded her just how selfish he was just hours earlier before she snuck off while he was sleep.

After Chico took care of his business in the bathroom, he washed his hand then he picked up his cell. It was his wife, Myriah. He loved her so, his heartbeat quickening as he found his wife sitting on the sofa. Her legs were wide open. Her satin, peanut butter skin against the bright pink lips she exposed with two fingers. It was like an exquisite painting. He couldn't get enough of it as she slowly worked her budding clitoris.

"Mmmhmm," she said before she dipped her finger inside of herself. She pulled it out and stuck it in her mouth, making a popping sound. She laughed as she watched him sit there in awe with his mouth open.

"What? You miss her? It's been like what, a month or so? You miss your pussy, papi?"

"Hell, fuck yeah. Let me see that pussy, Myriah. Spread it open some more," he told his wife, whipping his already erect penis out. Just that quickly, he forgot about Shonasia in the bedroom.

"Chi—" she started to say. She couldn't, watching him stroke his dick slow and hard.

"Yeah, mami. Now go do what papi told you to do. Then put two fingers in there and work them shits in and out."

She leaned back, giving him a closer view as she worked her center. It began to swish and leak from her self-imposed invasion. She then took her hand, lifted her breast, and sucked her nipple while fucking herself with two fingers. The more she licked and sucked, the harder he got.

"That's right, My," he said, calling her by her pet name. "Do that shit while you playing in papi's pussy."

He watched her stomach flex in and out as her muscles contracted. The small stretch marks across her belly created the most beautiful sight he'd ever seen. They were a reminder that she would forever be marked as a result of carrying his babies. It was his undying love for her and his babies that made him forget the rider Shona was to him. He loved her, but he was in love with Myriah, pleasuring himself at the sight of his wife's garden.

"Yessss," he hissed. "Oh, mami. Fuck, I can't wait to get home. I'm going to bend all that ass over and murder that pussy. You like that? You want me to suck that pussy and lick that ass from the back?"

"Unnn huh," she said, rapidly swirling her fingers around her now engorged clit. "Uhhhh, uh, uh. Ohhhh, mmmm."

Chico leaned up as if he were there. He stood up tall, imagining himself hitting it from the back. As he faced the shower, his back was to the door as they made fuck faces as they hissed and growled at each other. He was about to bust a good one when the bathroom door opened, followed by a loud outburst.

"Chico, what the hell?" Shona asked, covering her mouth when she saw Myriah's face on his cell's FaceTime.

Myriah immediately stopped and sat up, her eyes widening. She screamed before she dropped her cell on the floor.

"Fuck, Shonasia! Got damn!" he barked, realizing what had just happened. "This some bullshit!"

"Yes, this is some bullshit!" she shot back, her face flushed with embarrassment and her feelings hurt. "I knew I shouldn't have trusted shit you had to stay. The same old Chico. Fuck you, sorry ass bitch!"

She walked out and slammed the door. When he looked back at his cell, there sat his wife staring back at him silently crying. Her right arm was pressed firmly against her side as she stood rigid yet shaking.

As he began to plead, hoping she would listen to him, he watched her slowly raise her arm, revealing something shiny. It was a knife. She dropped to her knees, now wailing loudly. She was done.

After almost twenty years, he managed to make her feel that she still wasn't the one. For years she was the pretty slut, the pretty whore, until he wifed her and she couldn't take it anymore.

She placed the tip of the knife underneath her neck, asking him why repeatedly. He cried out, begging her to stop, but she reached forward and disconnected the call.

"How's the wife? Is her FaceTime still working?" Shona hissed, roughly pushing him off her as his dick flopped out of her. She couldn't believe she gave him the pussy after that. Not after she took off. Still, he found her that morning. She waited for an Uber at a nearby coffee shop.

Before she left, she wrote him a letter asking him to never contact her again. He was in a deep sleep, sleeping peacefully while she was in pain. She loved him with all her heart and in a matter of hours, he made her hate herself for loving him. Once again, he chose Myriah and she chose the side bitch role.

She bent over and kissed him. Her lips against his skin felt like hot coal causing her to frown once she did.

She shook her head, full of disgust before she slapped the shit out of him.

Whap!

"Fuck! Why the hell are you slapping me?" he snarled, his partially erect penis still out as he grabbed his face. Their sex permeated the air, making her even angrier.

"Because bitch, you are dead to me." Reaching in her pocket, she pulled out her knife. She was a killer, a stone-cold killer. He had taught her well but soon forgot. She concluded that only love could make you forget to protect yourself.

"Dead?" he repeated, unsure if he wanted to slap her back or fuck her into submission. "You're fucking bugging, ma," he told her, chuckling as his member softened completely.

"Oh yeah?" she said, quickly raising her knife to his throat. "Am I still bugging, you piece of shit? Back the fuck up!" she barked as he felt the knife prick his skin, causing him to flinch. He tucked his teeth with clenched fists, nodding his head.

"Shit. A'ight then," he whispered, fighting hard to maintain his composure.

If she were anyone else, he would've killed her, but she wasn't. No matter what she thought, he did love her. He did as she said, hearing the seriousness in her voice. His member was completely flaccid as he backed up, allowing her feet to rest fully on the ground. Her pretty pussy peeked at him, but he took that L, holding both hands in the air.

"Yeah, back the fuck up. Now, either we leave out this bitch bloody and on a gurney or walk out with you leaving me the fuck alone."

"You win, Shonasia," he said, gritting his teeth as he reached down and pulled his sweat pants up.

"Yeah, I did win. I dodged a fucking bullet the day you chose her. Remember, I'm not that bitch you raised. I'm the bitch you groomed."

In five hours, she was back in Miami heartbroken and alone. The new year was quickly approaching and she was done. No more Chico, no more love. She was done.

CHAPTER TWO

Present

P   "Mr. West, you have a call on line one," Jessica, his paralegal, advised him from her desk.

"Uh, can you take a message? I'm slammed with requests since Andre's indictment came down."

"Mr. West, you know that really is my job," she whispered. "I can handle that instead of all this administrative work you have me doing."

Rarely did he stress, but this was a case that could make or break him because it was high profile. Up until now, he'd never lost a case. Even if there was one to lose, he knew it couldn't be this one. Andre Perry, college roommate and frat brother, was facing a life sentence. This was a classic case of wrong place, wrong time, but with his DNA being on the victim's body and in the hotel room, Xander had his work cut out for him.

He enjoyed the company of women, having many sexual partners being the popular, athletic guy on campus over the years. But drugging and raping them, even leaving for dead wasn't something Andre would ever do.

"I know, I know. It's just—look, you're right," he said, sighing. He took off his glasses, rubbing his temple. His head was killing him. Jessica was damn good, but Andre deserved the best defense.

He'd depleted his savings and his home was in foreclosure. Xander never judged, growing up as a black man, so this wasn't just for Andre. This was for all of the black men unjustly accused. He knew that to be true and he'd be damned if he'd leave his boy to the wolves.

"I am, X," she whispered, calling him by his nickname. They mostly stuck with Mr. West when they were in the office, but to his friends and close family, he was X.

"I'll brief you on everything I have before I head out this afternoon, then it's yours. You know I take this kind of personal. He's like family," he said, full of frustration. "Who is it anyway?"

"It's Ms. Sampson," she replied, clearing her throat as she referenced his ex-girlfriend. Jessica would never admit to having a crush on her boss, but when it came to his ex-girlfriend, everyone hated her. Especially Jessica.

"Who, Avery? Damn," he said, resorting to a whisper. "Tell her I'm not here. Hell, anything you want." *This bitch is crazy,* he said to himself. "Did you remind George she has no personal nor professional reason for being in the building?"

"Yes, I have, but George is old. He's not putting a woman out of a building. Plus, he has a soft spot in his heart for her. Remember when her father helped his grandson's case get overturned?," she said, her voice a bit elevated now. "So George's not stopping her." .

The pain shot across his forehead, down the side of his face. "Fuck," he grunted

"Mr. West? Are you okay?" she asked, jumping up to come to his office.

"I'm good. Another headache, but I got something," he said, looking in his top drawer for his pain medication.

"You're getting them more and more. I told you what you need," she said, watching her line go dead. Her tone was laced with lust, not even trying to hide it.

So it worked in her favor he didn't hear it. She'd been crushing on X since he came to her high school to speak. He snatched her as an intern a few years later and the two had been working together ever since. Even if he played her to the left, often pretending like he couldn't date her, Jessica still cared about him. She hated he wouldn't let her just help him. Especially since Avery was calling again.

"What?" he asked, looking at his phone when she called him right back. X was about to call it a day if she hit him up one more time.

"Never mind," she said quietly, knowing he was pissed. "She hung up."

"Cool. We're good?"

"Uh, yeah," she said, feeling rejected.

"Jessica, we're good. Ignore that bitch. Let's just focus on work... please," he stressed.

He popped two pain pills in his mouth, grabbed a bottle of water, and chugged it down. He refused to get sidetracked, especially when it came to a woman. Avery fucked that up for him early on and Jessica was running a close second.

As he dove back into his work, he felt bad talking to her like that but he learned the hard way with Avery. If he didn't check something that bothered him head on, it was a recipe for disaster. This X, the one he became after love gone wrong, was coined as mean, even cold-hearted.

He had already grown up in a loveless, high performing home, so relationships usually mattered. He just didn't trust them and didn't want to. All he wanted to do is kick ass in the courtroom and fuck on a woman with no strings attached. Too bad there were no women around that could that, so here he was overdosing himself with work.

If asked, X would tell you he loved his mother. It was her need to stay with a spineless, cheating man called his father that made him dislike her most days. Still, Mrs. West was the type of woman he knew he'd want to marry one day. She was loyal, beautiful and a rider for her husband and family. He would gladly tell Judge Xander West Senior, with his piece of shit ass, he didn't t deserve her.

"Mr. West?" Jessica said, buzzing in again on the line.

"Yes, Jessica?"

"Sorry, but the alert popped up. Remember you told me to remind you about the Whittinghams' annual New Year's Eve Gala. Should I RSVP or not?"

"Yeah, sure."

Last year and the year before that, he'd gone with Avery. They were the talk of the prestigious law community. It didn't hurt that both of their fathers were well-regarded judges either. Hers at the Florida Supreme Court level, while his was a family court judge that oversaw foster care cases. "Me, plus one," he said, thinking of his sister, Reagan.

"Two?" she asked without even realizing it, her voice a bit elevated.

"Yes, Reagan and I," he said firmly. "She likes that kind of shit," he told her, laying his head back as he closed his eyes. Reagan was the life of any party. He needed that, anything but memories of Avery's cheating ass.

"Very well."

She released the line, irritated he was being short with her when it was Avery that couldn't take no for an answer. From the day they'd met, Avery went out of her way to prove her spot in his life. Jessica could remember days when she came in wearing nothing but a trench coat, screwing him loudly while she sat on the other side of the door. If it wasn't that, it was her mispronouncing her name on purpose.

X helped raise monies for inner city students, Jessica being one of them. So, of course, she was smitten by him. He took it as a little crush, but even crushes died out over time. Probably because he became one of the best defense attorneys in the nation, starting from the bottom at the Public Defender's Office until he opened up his own law firm.

To describe who X was, was impossible. He loved playing pool or video games. Even smoking a cigar with the boys as they sat around and talked shit, but he also loved literature. He would read for hours in between cases from street lit to mysteries. And when it came to how he looked, asked the ladies. He drove them wild no matter what he wore from a thousand dollar custom made suits to a pair of Balmain jeans, a plain white t-shirt and a fresh pair of Js against his butterscotch skin.

Then there was this dark side that sometimes spilled over into his personal life. X struggled most of his life and, truthfully, he still struggled. When that happened, anyone on the end of that was in the path of a lunatic.

He thought his cure to hoeing in college came in the form of Avery Sampson. They'd met at a law conference in DC. At first, she was beyond a breath of fresh air. She was intelligent, gorgeous and fuckable —a complete package. Standing at 5'11" with long legs, she had a sleek shape similar to one of a runway model.

Her full, yet firm cheekbones complemented by her dark brown, doe-shaped eyes and full lips were nothing short of amazing. Her skin complexion, almost akin to milk chocolate, was stunning. In fact, many would say Avery was damn near perfect until they realized how damaged she was on the inside like he did. He wondered why she didn't have many friends, but once he did, it was too late. He was all in, making excuses for her rude ass until the real her showed up.

Not only was she on Jessica's radar, but Reagan's, too.

His sister, like X, had been exposed to the finer things in life, but she was wild. She smoked like she had a built in chimney and drank most men out of every bottle of liquor sent their way. She loved to party and did, resulting in that drinking problem she had.

Still, X loved his sister while Avery used every chance she got to exclude her from his life. Reagan wasn't too fond of Jessica either, but they had a common enemy. That was Avery. That alone was enough to tolerate each other but Reagan had her eye on Jessica, too.

"Mr. West?" Jessica buzzed in, interrupting him a third time.

"Shit," he huffed before he answered. "Yes, Jessica?"

"George thinks he's spotted her, but he's not too sure. He seemed iffy to me. Told you he's no snitch," she all but said, mumbling. "Anyway, want me to lock the door?"

"Naw," he told her, checking to see if he had his 9-millimeter with him. He wasn't going to shoot her, but he didn't mind scaring the shit out of her. Name brand clothes didn't kill people. People did and he'd do what he had to do if it came down to it. Avery knew it, too.

CHAPTER THREE

It had been three years. Three years since Shona left her broken heart in the dark, dirty alley in New York. To many, she was fine, but during times like this, she remembered she wasn't.

"Merry Christmas to me," Shona whispered to herself, staring at the ceiling.

Her heart felt heavy as if something was missing. Sad thing was that nothing was missing if you knew her real life. This was how she woke up just about every Christmas. Just her and her alone with her thoughts.

She could fake it and pretend to be happy or sulk, but that was too much work. So, she chose to not feel anything, throwing herself somewhat into a festive mood. There was no Santa when she was a child and she never pretended there was. There wasn't a soul she could remember that ever cared, growing up in foster care, so she chose not to dwell on it, coming up with her own tradition.

It was Christmas Eve, just before midnight. Instead of opening up a gift or two like some families, she kicked off Christmas with breakfast at midnight. She'd go all out, even making it fancy for her and her baby sister, Kaleela.

She knew Kaleela was already up, hearing her sing "Silent Night" by the O'Jays.

"Ah, hell," she said and frowned, hearing her sing all off key. She could tell Kaleela's lips were intimately wrapped around a bottle of liquor. It was probably Hennessey, her favorite, as she howled loudly.

Both were the product of societal ills, when crack consumed your mother making the streets and an unknown face your father. It's all they'd known for the most part. Well Shona at least since Kaleela was just a baby. By the time she was old enough to know what was going on, Shona did as much as she could to make life normal for her.

In fact, Shona would make stories up just to make her feel good, but most were recorded lies she wrote down. She'd sit Kaleela on her lap, pretending that they lived in a big beautiful house with the prettiest mother in the whole wide world.

With no one to care for them, they stayed in the system until Shona met Chico one day at a corner store. She was sixteen. In no time, she was cooking his dope and giving him her body in exchange for the heart he never fully gave her.

She sucked her teeth thinking about New York but as she warned him, he did just what she asked, never reaching out. She was glad, too. She knew herself. Just one touch and taste of him and she'd be right back where she was.

Turning on the shower after slipping on her shower cap, Shona silently cried under the steady stream of water that hit her face. This was the only time she gave herself permission to cry about their life because as soon as Kaleela was around, she made it her business to keep her game face on.

Hearing Kaleela now scream an awful rendition of Chris Brown's "This Christmas," she hurried out of the shower.

"That damn girl is about to kill herself," she said, quickly drying herself off. After finishing up her hygiene, she slipped into a silly Hello Kitty onesie she found in the mall. Before she exited, she stopped and scrunched up her nose in the mirror. She made a blowfish face, feeling older than she looked.

She had baby face and honey brown eyes, all from her mother just like her skin complexion. She had one picture, just one she kept that now sat in her top drawer. Anytime she wondered what her children might look like, she'd grab that picture.

Kaleela, a shade lighter, had more of a slender face with doe-shaped eyes. Unlike her sister, she refused to get all dolled up using moisturizer of any kind. She was a natural beauty with thin lips that naturally curled when she smiled.

While hard on the outside, being the prettiest stud Shona had ever seen, Kaleela was unapologetically a whore. She loved strippers and pussy by the pound, literally.

"Hey, K baby. Feeling good, huh?" Shona said to her baby sister as she entered the living room, admiring her sister's beauty.

She nodded her head, lifting her bottle up as a toast and smiled. Shona laughed and shook her head. She couldn't drink without eating, but Kaleela went hard on a empty or full stomach. It didn't matter.

"Look at you," she sang, admiring Kaleela's wheelchair. "Gotcha wheels all decorated like you some Black Santa. Where are you going?" she teased.

She looked at the spray-painted wheels on her wheelchair. They were red and green finished off with a silver, cotton-like streamer woven throughout the spokes. Kaleela chewed the inside of her jar, electing not to respond. Instead, she threw her head back and gulped down the brown liquor. She liked it all, dark and light, but that dark made her do some strange things, causing Shona to look at eye out the side of her eye.

"Ahhhh, this some good shit," she then replied, holding it up to Shona's face.

"Soooo, no thank you," she said, turning the music down just a little. "I guess we just ignore folks and what not."

She figured it was the wheelchair, a reminder of what led them out of the game. Before then, they were unstoppable. While Shona was Chico's bitch, Kaleela's team drew in the most fiends and the most money. If anyone threatened that, bodies dropped with no hesitation. When you heard Kaleela's name, most times somebody was dying.

Anyone looking at Kaleela knew she wasn't wrapped tight. In fact, normal fell off the register right after birth. Ever since then, her gangster mentality festered in her blood, bobbing her head up and down. It was like she was sitting in a Maserati instead of a wheelchair in her all-black Adidas sweat suit.

"I'on feel like saying shit. I'm chilling and drinking." Shona watched the liquor dribble down her chin. Kaleela caught it with the back of her hand, trying to catch every drop.

She then broke out in song, lifting the bottle in the air. *"And this Christmassss, will beeeee, a very special Christmassssss for meeeeee. Ba da da da da da da da daaaaaa!"*

With their family history, Shona knew drinking was the last thing Kaleela should be doing, but she felt helpless at times when it came to helping her. She had legs that worked. Kaleela didn't. There wasn't a day that went by she didn't wish it were her instead, so there she sat and allowed her sister to drink her sorrows away.

"So what happened to your favorite Charlie Brown Christmas show?" Shona asked her, sitting on a soft, leather lounge chair.

"I'on know," she replied, shrugging her shoulders. "Shit like twenty years old and it's stupid. What forty-year-old manboy still playing with a damn dog anyway? That's whack as fuck." Kaleela laughed, then burped before punching her chest.

Shona knew it was the alcohol, especially if Kaleela wasn't watching the *Charlie Brown Christmas* special. Like breakfast, Kaleela had been watching that since she was old enough to know it was coming on. Even if they had to steal a TV, Shona made sure she got a chance to watch it.

Kaleela then cocked to the side, shaking her head as she stared at her older sister.

"What? Why are you looking at me like that?"

"Yo, tell me why in all of *the hell* you are wearing that tight ass Hello Kitty shit?" Kaleela asked, laughing before another burp followed.

"A'ight then," Shona said with a slight attitude, getting up. She was just as in her feelings, but being the bigger person was starting to wear off. "Let me go before I say something that will change your whole vibe. Dumb ass broad," she huffed, deciding to walk away.

"Move the fuck on then. Being all extra sensitive. Period must be about to come on?"

"You know, I understand you could have been somewhere else with someone else. But damn, can we at least have a day—wait, what about a moment without it being all about you? It's always about you," she told her, crossing her arms. "And while you're here diagnosing my ass, go get yourself fixed."

"Tuh, why me? My ass ain't dressed up like a thirty-year-old hoe posing as a toddler," Kaleela shot back, full of the giggles.

"Naw, but you are dressed up like LL Cool J ready to make a comeback from the nursing home," Shona clapped back and chuckled. "Yeah, lick them thin ass lips."

"Bet a bitch ain't complaining," she shot back, waving her off.

"Whatever," Shona told her, choosing to not argue with someone who was damn near drunk.

Kaleela closed her eyes. She didn't have time to discuss feelings and how fucked up her life was. That shit was getting old, too old. She'd rather drink and was feeling good before her sister showed up. Shona watched her face twitch, knowing if she didn't walk, this would be a fight. But when Kaleela mumbled "fuck you, hoe", she roughly snatched the bottle out her hand, turning on her heels as she headed towards the kitchen.

"Aye, why you took my shit?" she snapped, whipping around to follow her.

"Because you're talking stupid," Shona boldly replied, leaning down in her face. "As soon as you get drunk, you don't care about anything or anyone except this right here and those bitches. Stop numbing and dumbing your feelings down and sucking their little pussies, girl. Live in the motherfucking real world. This is the real world!" she all but yelled, ready to light her little sister's ass up. "And this right here is going to kill you if those hoes don't. Grow the fuck up, K."

The entire time Shona fussed, Kaleela breathed heavily, giving her a deathly stare. "What I do with my mouth and their pussy is my business. I keep telling you to stop with all this parental shit. And I'm grown!" she yelled, clapping her hands. "The fuuuuck!"

"What, you think I'm scared of you? Clap your fucking hands. I don't care," she said slowly, emphasizing each word as she watched Kaleela's every move.

That wheelchair may have slowed her down, but Shona knew her sister. She was a got damn beast on wheels with swift hands and no conscience. She'd raised her to be that way to survive. That wheelchair didn't do anything but make her harder, more rebellious.

"Shona?" she said, warning her as she lifted both brows.

"Don't no Shona me. Don't think because you're in a wheelchair, I won't beat that ass. *I'm still that bitch*. Ain't nothing changed but where the fuck I live and how I get this money," she snarled, her chinky eyes damn near closed.

Kaleela sat up easy and slow. She then leaned on her knees, pulling on the end of her nose. All she could see or feel was murder while Shona talked that hot shit.

"You know if you were a bitch in the streets, your chest would have been decorated by now with your Cheech and Chong looking ass," Kaleela told her, looking at her with squinted eyes. "But I know what your problem is," she said, sitting back and smiling. "You need some dick in your life."

"Fuck you," Shona growled, fighting hard to hold back the tears that began to form.

"Yeah, that's it," Kaleela said, smiling. She knew she was getting somewhere now. If she was in a fucked up place, Shona might as well be, too. "Maybe somebody needs to suck on *your pussy*. Bitch, you're deprived. Ain't had a man in years and the one you had still wasn't yours, shorty," Kaleela said with much satisfaction, breaking Shona down all the more.

Before Kaleela could blink her eyes, Shona whipped out her hot pink .22, aiming it front and center. Her chest, heaving up and down, kept time as she wrestled with her mental to give her sister a pass. She knew Kaleela was fucked up in the head, but so was she. The minute she bought that outfit, she got a built in pouch added just to carry.

Besides, it was Christmas time and no neighborhood was safe. But truthfully, she'd been sleeping with her heat for years. Her finger felt itchy, silently telling her to pull. Kaleela rolled closer, surprising her when she grabbed her hand and placed the mouth of her bitch on her forehead.

"Kill me. Yeah," she laughed lowly, her hand firmly wrapped around

Shona's. "Why the fuck am I here anyway? What purpose do I serve, Shona? I'm in your fucking way. So do it," she growled.

Shona started to cry, shaking her head no. If it wasn't for her baby sister, it was she who would have killed herself by now. There were many days, Kaleela was her one and only reason for waking up and facing a world that didn't seem to love her back.

"Yeah, talk that bullshit now," she hissed, trying to grab her bottle out of Shona's other hand. Shona closed her eyes, praying for God to quiet her mind soon snapped out of it when Kaleela whipped her 9-millimeter out her ankle strap, pointing it at her.

Shona smiled a wicked grin, then dragged her tongue across her teeth. Her gun was still trained on Kaleela who was egging her on.

"Yeah, that's the bitch I know. 'Bout time," Shona laughed wickedly. "All this emotional shit is not us. Glad you finally showed the fuck up. Understand you better kill me with that first pull, because you know my bang is official. I'll squeeze one out before you blink," Shona hissed, referring to her piece she named Pink Lady.

Kaleela now felt her hand shaking. No bitch could ever make her as mad like her sister and she not do anything. She felt her eyes tearing up, rage rattling all throughout her body. Usually the only way to fix that kind of high was to spill blood, but she couldn't spill what they both shared.

"Fuck!" Kaleela screamed, slapping herself in the face over and over. Shona popped her in the middle of her forehead, knocking her back as she dropped her piece. "Damn it, Shona. Fuck!"

"That's right. Stop acting all psychotic, K," she said, squinting her eyes at her as she fought to catch her breath. "Fucking up my Christmas for real."

"Bitch, you're the crazy one!" Kaleela told her, spittle flying everywhere "Just leave me the hell alone! Let me die!"

Shona felt awful, hearing her sister want death like that's all she deserved. She almost fell out of her chair, trying to get away. "I feel sorry for you," she laughed and cried at the same time. "Guess who's stuck with me? Your ass, but now you hate me. Hate my crippled ass. Just let me go, Shona," she wailed, punching both legs.

Shona couldn't believe what she'd just heard. Kaleela was the strongest person in life to her. She'd go crazy if she wasn't around, dropping to her knees in front of her as she grabbed her by one hand then pulled her chair up.

"I can't, I won't," she told her sister, then pulled her body to hers. "Stop it. It's me that's fucked up. You're right. I did fuck up. I'm lonely, but guess what? I'll be okay. Just don't try to leave me, K. Please." She laughed when she said that, feeling stupid.

"Aw hell, girl," Kaleela said, trying to get her out of her face. "You're tripping, bitch."

"But you love this bitch, don't you?" Shona asked her, leaning in as she stole a quick kiss on her cheek.

"Stop all that," Kaleela mumbled, wiping her cheek.

"Nope."

Affection wasn't something neither showed in a healthy way, but what they did show was real. She regretted a lot of things in her life, but never protecting and caring for her sister.

"Whatever," Kaleela mumbled, wiping her face. "You don't need no fucking cripple around."

"Yes, I do," she said, reaching up to help her clean her face with the back of her hand. "We gotta do something, K baby. Maybe rehab."

"I'on need no rehab, Shona. Those people won't like me. Nope, I don't wanna go," she said pouting, looking lost as she rubbed the top of her head, sniffling.

"Hey," Shona said softly, holding her hands. "This is not my Kaleela talking. Girl, you've been making friends since before you could talk. We always got our asses beat because you talked so much shit. Don't act like you don't remember," Shona teased, snickering. "That last foster home lady, what's her name?"

"Miss Cooney with her looney ass. Bitch stayed jumping at the smallest sound." Kaleela quickly replied with a smile. "I'm telling you that hoe was bipolar. Them voices in that bitch head got us in trouble. Not me," she said and chuckled, her face still wet as she wiped the last of her tears away.

"Girl, whatever." She stood and smiled, looking at her baby sister. Kaleela, even mad and fucked up like she was, was still beautiful to her. "Anyway, after the new year, let's go check a few rehabs. I promise if you're not feeling it, we'll keep looking until we find one that you do like."

Kaleela's lips trembled, but she nodded her head agreeing.

"A'ight, sis. I'll go," she told her, backing up. "Holla at me when breakfast is done."

She pulled a blunt out of her pocket, ready to blow one. Neither were allowed to smoke in the house, but Shona was willing to make an exception. In fact, Shona only smoked when they went out and that was almost never.

"Yup, I already know," Kaleela said, going to the back near the patio.

"See, I was going to say it's okay today. Always trying to think for me," Shona told her. Just that quickly, they were back at it again.

Kaleela couldn't believe she agreed to go to rehab, taking a pull as she felt the smoke coursing through her lungs. Her therapy was fucking hoes, smoking and drinking while Shona chose to bury hers, acting like life was good. "Shit, her ass needs rehab too. Rehab from hating on how I treat my bitches," she mumbled to herself.

Shona heard her but walked off with her .22 to get breakfast started. She tossed the bottle in the trash and sighed. "Let me get rid of all of them," she said to herself, opening the bottom cabinet were they kept all the liquor. One by one, she took out every bottle from Hennessey to Patron. Then she moved on to the wine and champagne.

She reached down, grabbing the first one she saw, and gasped. It was a bottle of Andre' Brut California. Her body stiffened, remembering the night she got it but never opened it. She sighed, remembering she gave Kaleela strict orders to trash it once they left the crew over six years ago. It was before Kaleela got shot.

"Dang, Kaleela. I should have known you can't part with a bottle of anything." Truthfully, she wanted to be the one to get rid of it, but she couldn't. It felt too much like letting go. Still, after everything that happened in New York, she still hadn't. She just was better at hiding it.

She smiled, picking it up and holding it with both hands. Chico had purchased a case right after a big merger with this Mexican cartel out on the west coast. It was symbolic of them taking over California.

The empire they were building was expanding now from coast to coast, including high-powered guns after linking up with some Haitians deep in the gun game. And like always, more money meant more problems, starting with Chico and his rather friendly dick.

While everyone was toasting, Chico had Shona cornered off upstairs in an exclusive VIP section. She was bent over, titties hanging out and all as he hit it from the back. Shona was in her zone, bouncing on his dick like a basketball while Trina's "The Baddest Bitch" boomed loudly throughout the room.

With each bounce, he popped her ass and dug deeper into her slippery slope. He showed no mercy, delivering a killer stroke that made her legs go numb. And like the good girl she was whenever it came to him, she took it like a champ.

By the time the lights came on, she was pinned up against the wall in a split with all of his babies running out of her and down her ass onto the floor. With no shame, he tongued her down and kept pumping until she came once more, collapsing with her legs in the crook of his arms.

Feeling all these emotions as she stared at it, she quickly tossed it in the trashcan and slammed the lid down.

She then threw herself right in, whipping up the pancake batter after she put the grits on the stove and the bacon in the oven. She pulled out a bowl of seasoned shrimp. They would be last since it would be sautéed, ready to eat within minutes after everything was done. As she poured the batter onto the skillet, she stopped when she thought she heard something. The music was still on, but that sound was different.

"Probably her ass throwing stuff around in her room," she mumbled to herself about Kaleela. "That damn girl is about to drive me to drink." Then she heard it again. It was series of rapid taps on the front door. Somebody was there.

"Un uh, K!" she yelled, taking the skillet off the hot eye of the stove. "Not today! Tell them tricks to spend the holiday with their niggas or hell, how about their kids!"

The last thing she wanted was to hear was some bitch screaming while Kaleela's head was nestled between her legs.

"Kaleela! Who is that?" she yelled once more, until she heard a sound that could make a room full of niggas pause.

Click, click.

She immediately reached for hers, taking off. Kaleela aim's was deadly but without knowing who was at the door, she took no chances, rounding the corner with her adrenaline at an all-time high.

She halted, almost tripping over her own feet when she saw who it was. It was him—Chico. She clenched her fist, tightly gripping her .22. There he was in all of his ghettofied glory showing off his ripped, tatted arms as he wore an orange Lacoste polo shirt and a pair of dark wash jeans slightly hanging off his hips.

His hooded brown eyes, barely visible, made an appearance as he took off his fitted UM cap just in time to catch Kaleela. Shona almost panicked, realizing Kaleela must have forgotten she could not walk from all the liquor in her system.

"Oh shit!" she screamed while Kaleela yelled, "Chicooooooo!" It all happened so fast, that she forgot to move, her feet feeling cemented to the floor

"Whoa, girl!" he said, laughing as he hoisted her. "Your lil' ass heavy!" Kaleela shook her head no, crying uncontrollably as he patted her back. She couldn't help it. She hadn't seen him in years, coupled with feeling bad about her fight with Shona.

"Shhhh. Come on now, K baby," he whispered.

He continued to rub the back of her head as she held on to him like a little child. Her head was tucked so deep into the crook of his neck, he had a full view of one of the prettiest girls he had ever met in his life.

His eyes latched on to hers, but unlike his, hers were icy and cold. As he comforted Kaleela, kissing her on the top of her head, his baby browns began to wear Shona down. She wanted to maintain her cold-hearted stance, but her tear ducts betrayed her.

"Shit," she mumbled, tossing her head back as she squeezed her eyes tightly. She wiped her eyes before she dropped her head down again. The last thing she wanted was for him to see her cry.

When she did, it was like he was eye fucking her. His eyes told a story, but so did hers. His were lazy and soft, not to mention full of sorrow. Hers were not. They were immovable, now showing no emotion short of being misty which could mean anything. She lowkey felt good seeing the pain in his.

He'd been debating since New York three years earlier if he should come through. He'd always known where she lived. This was still his city, getting the code to her gated community for easy access. He was even offered a key. He declined, however, somewhat wanting to play fair by knocking on the door instead.

The only thing different this year was he turned his life over to God. He'd not only given up the streets, but he was now in the church. He wasn't a holy roller, but he and his wife had been going to church. She'd even had another child since the time he saw Shona in New York.

Since then, not only was he a man after God's heart, he was madly in love with his wife. They were three kids deep now, and he was ready to pump more in her. Still, his heart longed for Shona at times, hoping she would render him what he needed from her. That was forgiveness.

Like an addict, the first step to recovery was admitting your dysfunction. His was definitely being selfish, and disloyal to women who did nothing but loved him, starting with Shona.

"I miss you," Kaleela whimpered, after finding her voice again.

"Pfft," Shona huffed. "That's a damn shame," she muttered under her breath, feeling betrayed.

Kaleela had a right to love who she loved, but acting like he didn't abandon the both of them years ago made her sick to her stomach. Then there was that stunt in New York. She cringed thinking about it.

"I miss you, too, K baby."

Kaleela felt good hearing that, leaning back and smiling. She released his neck, forgetting she couldn't even stand on her own once again.

"Hold on, girl. Slow down," he said, laughing as he caught her again. He smelled the liquor, so he knew she was tipsy. "No more for your ass. Still taking it to the head, I see," he told her.

"I got something for your head," she shot back, patting her piece against the side of her leg.

"Now that's the K baby I know. Niggas ate bullets once you came on the scene full of emotion. Around here crying," he said, smiling. "My baby girl done went and got soft on me."

"Naw, boss man," Kaleela said smirking, almost feeling alive like old times. "Just some shit in my eye."

"A'ight," Chico said, "Let's call it a truce then."

He leaned down to hug her one more time. Just that quickly, she felt all giddy as they swayed left and right. It didn't hurt he got a good view of Shona's pussy print right in his face as she stood behind them. If he didn't know any better, she was doing it on purpose.

"You wish," Shona said lowly, watching him undress her with his eyes with her own piece still in her hand.

His chest tightened, hearing her reject him, but he expected that. Yet, he was still there and he knew Shona. If she really wanted him gone, he'd be carried away on his back by now.

Choosing to ease his way in without conflict, he threw all of his attention Kaleela's way. "You're good now?"

"I guess," she said, shrugging. She couldn't believe he was there, but knew her sister probably wouldn't let him stay.

"You guess?" he spat, a nervous laugh followed. She gave him a nod, feeling the heat from her sister's eyes boring into her back from behind.

"C'mere," he teased, bending as he playfully tried to lift her up. "I'll body slam yo' ass. You know how Chico do it." She tried mushing his face, but he kissed her on the cheek. She kissed him back, putting him in a headlock.

While they wrestled, Chico stole at glance at Shona. He watched her bite her lip, wishing his were on hers. He was saved, but his flesh was still tempted. Kaleela yoked him one good time, but not before he saw a tear slip down her cheek. Then he remembered why he was there again. He needed forgiveness.

"Yoooo," he yelled, pulling himself away and stepping back. "You got it, K."

Although he was enjoying this exchange, he couldn't lie and say Kaleela's happy response to him being there was enough. He was just about to speak to Shona, but she shook her head no, holding one hand up.

"Shonasia," he whispered in that same raspy voice that fucked with her mental every time. "Baby, let me talk to you." He reached his hand out, just above Kaleela's head. She whipped her head around, confused when she saw her sister crying. Shona never cried, at least not in front of her.

"Shit," she mumbled, looking at Kaleela. "Shit, shit, shit!" She wanted to walk away, but she couldn't, hearing his words play over and over in her head. They were like weights, holding her feet down.

She was loyal, always had been. Even now she was, not putting it out there how he did her in New York. He could tell Kaleela didn't know, knowing God had granted him some grace in her eyes. If she did, that greeting he got would have been a set up for his takedown.

"Shonasia, para, ma. No Llores," he whispered, telling her to stop crying in Spanish.

She closed her eyes, her heart fluttering like the weak bitch it was. Even her stomach started to rumble at the sound of his voice. *Shit, I'm in trouble,* she said to herself. All the while, Kaleela sat by looking up at the two of them.

Taking a chance, Chico leaned over her, slowly pushing her chair back just enough until his face rested immediately in front of Shona's. Her lips quivered just a little, but she didn't move. Even with her eyes closed, she could still feel him.

He waited, carefully and slowly for any sign of resistance but when he got none, he went for it. A faint smile appeared, praying she wouldn't move as he inched closer. Finally, their lips connected.

He slipped his hand behind the back of her neck and pulled her in to his mouth. She sighed, parting her mouth just enough for him to slide his tongue in. He then wrapped his juicy lips around hers, sucking on her bottom lip. A tickled Kaleela snickered as their kiss deepened.

Deciding not to push her any further, he pulled away and whispered, "Bebé, lo jodí. Por favor, déjame volver a entrar." He was admitting he was wrong, seeking her forgiveness. Even the kiss was wrong, but damn it if his heart wasn't in the right place. He just wanted her to heal and free her to love again. "So, do you forgive me? For everything, since way back in the day until now?"

"Shit, she better!" Kaleela shouted, understanding Spanish just as much as Shona did. "Her ass ain't had no dick in years! Bruh, you better getcho bitch! She's mean and grouchy as hell!"

Chico fell out, laughing. Kaleela was still crazy as hell, but he wouldn't change a thing about her. He dapped her up like old times, before reaching down to grab her piece.

"Next time you pull this shit on me, you better wet my ass up," he told her, before pinching her nose. "Don't let no motherfucker pop up unannounced and you not lay his ass down, K baby. You're tripping," Chico told her, wagging his finger at her. She grinned since he's the one that started calling her that. She was and would always be his "K baby".

Kaleela waved him off, tapping her ankle strap. "Shid, whatever," she murmured, knowing he was right.

She did know better, but she was glad she didn't pop him. To her, Chico was like God on earth, gracing the hood and now her part of town like it was all his.

"And your ass, too," he said to Shona. "I don't care if I bought you that little pink damn toy. You better pump that shit, woman."

"Whatever," Shona replied, turning around to give him her back. "Fuck you and you," she said, referring to the both of them.

She walked off, swishing all that ass he loved even more from this view. Truthfully, she was glad he pulled away. If it lasted a second longer, she knew his dick would soon be resting in her mouth or worse, her pussy.

CHAPTER FOUR

Tonight was X's pool night with his boys. It was three of them. Ace, Tooley and Gator. Out of the three, X was the closest to Ace as they grew up together. They both met Tooley and Gator in college. They were all thriving in their profession, but didn't let what they did for a living dictate how they vibed in their downtime. Pool night proved to be one of their most profitable nights, often betting against each other. He knew if he cancelled again, he owed each of them five hundred dollars.

Kicking himself for getting distracted, he plowed back into his research as he worked diligently to build a solid defense case. "I know I'm missing something," he said to himself, turning to his computer to look up one more case.

He heard his doorknob turning, startling him, which quickly evolved into an attitude. "Oh, you," he said, watching his father walk in like he owned his firm.

"Xander West, is that a way to greet your father?" he asked him, even though he didn't wait for an answer. "Need I remind you that where respect is given, it is also received?"

Here comes the bullshit, he thought to himself, hearing his father preach something he didn't apply himself.

"What's up, Dad? Is everything good with Mom? Reagan?" he asked, appeasing him just a little to get him out of there faster.

"You would know about that daughter of mine. I mean, she barely speaks to me, but your mother is fine last I checked. It's you that I am worried about."

His father rocked back and forth on his feet, a smirk on his face as he waited for his one and only son to remember.

"Damn, I forgot," X said, sighing as he took a deep breath.

They were doing this weekly lunch thing. His mother proposed it, hoping it would smooth things over as they approached the new year. Wanting to see her somewhat happy, X agreed, but today he wasn't feeling it.

They were alike yet different in so many ways. In fact, if one stared at the two of them, the resemblance was uncanny short of their age difference and his father's salt and pepper hair.

The only thing X got from his mother was her fine lips, while Reagan looked exactly like her, being damn near white. His mother was one shade darker than the average Caucasian person, coming from a biracial background. Between the two of them, he and his sister looked exactly how their parents did when they were their age.

Their mother's father, a well-off Jewish man, fell in love with her black woman who worked for his family. After marriage and four kids later, his mother Nora clung to status. Her younger sisters, however, proudly embraced their black side. It was because of them, X and Reagan never forgot where they came from.

"You look tired," his father said, looking around at all the plaques on his wall. He knew his son was great at what he did, but what X didn't do well, in his opinion, was leave his street mentality and the people there behind.

"And?" X asked, seeing his father's visit going south very quickly.

He felt a feud brewing, but so did his father as he smiled at him. X stared at his father's short and wavy cropped hair. X had missed his weekly haircut, he remembered, running his hands through his. His father's smooth skin and soft, brown eyes seemed to smile the angrier he got.

"And you need rest. It's clearly why you can't remember a thing.

What, work's gotten to be a bit much for you?" he chuckled, which was short-lived, looking down on X with disapproval. "You know you've been distracted, son. Heck, even Avery called me yesterday wanting to know if everything was okay. She told me she's been calling only to get uh, uh your secretary Jennifer on the line."

"It's paralegal, Dad. And it's Jessica, not Jennifer," he seethed, sitting up. "And why the fuck is she calling you? You're hitting that too?"

His father laughed, watching his son unravel. He enjoyed how mere words drove him insane.

"Son, I'm married, but if I was hitting that—" he emphasized with quoted fingers. "—trust that her calls to you would have never even started," his father said laughed, shaking his head. "You give these women way too much power," he bent down, telling his son. X's jaw twitched, trying to remember this was his father.

"Here it comes," X grunted lowly, ready to get this over with.

"No, I'm promise you, I came in peace. All I will say is if you are enjoying the benefits of being with a woman, at least let it be a woman like Avery. She's nice to look at and probably a nice piece of ass, but you wouldn't know that. I heard you're even turning that down," his father revealed with some sense of satisfaction. "Certainly not a West man."

"Being a West man is not what makes me. And pussy that runs like it's in a marathon doesn't either," he told him, slowly standing up.

He clenched his fists, feeling his head pound even harder. He was tired of this little game, ready to have Jessica bail him out of jail for whipping his father's ass.

"Sit down, please," his father warned him. His voice was soft, deep, and even. He was ready for whatever his son's fury brought, but he did his dirt behind closed doors unlike his son to his knowledge. "I'm here for lunch. Remember? Or maybe we should just cancel. Your choice. People have choices. I do and so do you."

X bit down really hard, trying hard not to disappoint his mother.

"So, you'd be okay if Mom chose to cheat? I mean, since you are endorsing choices, maybe she should choose to be a hoe like the one you're throwing up in my face," he hissed, backing up to put some space in between them.

"Xander!" his father barked. "One, I'm still your father. And two…" he paused and laughed, rubbing the bridge of his nose. "Your mother knows her place. That also means who she belongs to."

"You're sure about that?" X replied quickly, smiling as he thought about Mr. John. He was the neighbor next door. His wife died a few years ago. X's mother, being the nurturer she was, often made sure Mr. John had food. Especially on Sundays.

"Oh, I'm very sure. See, I never have to worry about her roaming or another man getting her attention. When you do what you're supposed to do, another man would rather perish than mess with yours. And riddle me this. What do you think I would do if I found out another man knows how your mother's pussy felt, huh?" he asked, then laughed a loud, hideous laugh that dug at his son's core.

"Out," X spoke lowly, pointing to the door.

"Ah, come on, son. Loosen up. I'm—"

"Out," he said once again, walking around his desk as he loosened up his tie. "I would beat your ole ass, but the respect you speak of I still have some of it *for my mother*. Speak on her again like she's some common bitch, and they'll be carrying you out, Judge West, and I mean that shit."

He waved his hand at his son, smiling.

"Think it's a joke?" he asked his father, loosening his cufflinks.

"There it is. That street side you love to portray. "

"Those streets made me and you, but you're the one that seemed to have forgotten where you came from. You married Mom who pretty much passes for white, got into a few of those good ole boy clubs and now you think you're not black. Fuck with the right one and they'll remind you."

"Let's pretend like today didn't happen, son," he pretty much threatened his son as he prepared to leave. He wasn't sure how much more he could take before the two of them were in an actual physical brawl. "And don't forget to RSVP for the Whittinghams' annual New Year Gala. Your mother worked very hard this year. I would like nothing more than for you to come out," he said, acting as if their word sparring had never occurred.

X wanted to tell him to fuck off, but he couldn't as Jessica buzzed in again. "Damn, what the hell is up today?"

"It's called get control over your house. I can't tell if I'm in a law office or a zoo, Xander," he said, reaching for the door.

"Mr. West?"

"Jessica, it better be good. I do not want any more calls for the rest of the day. I can't get anything done."

"But you said—"

"Oh, for God's sake, X! Let me in! You have me standing out here like some thug!" Avery barked after snatching the phone out of Jessica's hand. "I've been calling, texting, even emailing you and you cannot stop for a second to even respond!

After I gave you the best three years of my life, this is what I get? You got your little thuggette security screening everything that comes through here. Does she know how long you can go before you pass out, too?"

He looked at his father who appeared to be enjoying himself. He disconnected the line, grabbing both sides of his head. His father sighed, walking over to him and touching his shoulder. He flinched just a little, looking at him as he was ready to annihilate him. "Another headache, son?"

"Why? Would that make you feel better or do you actually care?"

"Oh, I care," he told him, walking towards the door and finally opening it. "I care way more than you know. One day you will thank me. Take care of yourself. You need it, son."

Once he stepped outside of his office, there stood a frustrated Avery whose tight smile became even tighter. "Apparently she cares too, but I guess we're not underprivileged enough to get some of your precious time," he said before acknowledging Avery's presence.

"Avery, my dear. It's lovely seeing you again. Tell your father we must do a round of golf and soon. Oh, and forgive my son. I can tell he's not getting serviced properly," he said, looking at Jessica and then X. "Xander, let's do dinner if that suits your rather busy schedule. I'll be sure to tell your mother," he suggested, kissing Avery on the cheek as he finally left.

"Don't," X warned her, as she placed one foot on the other side of his door. "I still owe you a fucking ass whooping."

Before she could protest, he walked towards his door and slammed it in her face.

CHAPTER FIVE

I t was six o'clock in the morning and the sun had just cracked the sky. Just an hour earlier, Chico woke up on the sofa staring at Kaleela sprawled across on the reclining love seat. He smiled watching her with her mouth wide open. It wasn't a sight he was used to seeing, but she was so cute to him as he watched dried up drool on the side of her mouth.

Sitting up, he stretched and looked around. A few red cups and an empty bottle of Grey Goose were nearby. They'd stepped out to grab one while Shona stayed back to cook breakfast. When they returned, his heart swelled seeing a nice spread of freshly cut fruit and blueberry muffins while she flipped pancakes and scrambled eggs.

He watched her move around the kitchen effortlessly, quickly putting on a pot of grits before she tossed some shrimp in a skillet. The Shona he knew was never domestic, but after cooking dope for years, he figured she finally got around to learning how to actually cook a meal, and she didn't disappoint.

Before they knew it, they were laughing and talking trash about old times, being sure to stay away from anything that spoke on their past situation. Occasionally, he would ask questions about her nonexistent love life, but Shona would quickly change the subject to Kaleela's whoreish ways.

She wasn't ready to discuss what life had been like for the past few years since they'd last seen each other. She wanted to just relax in the moment and chill. So, they did until they all fell off to sleep.

Before he got up, Shona slipped off to her room and cried herself to sleep. It hurt scrolling through his wife's Facebook page filled with pictures of the cutest kids. His son, almost eighteen, looked just like him while their daughter Storm, the cutest six-year-old, was a lighter, tanned version of her mother. Then their youngest, CJ, was the nicest blend of the two, stealing Shona's heart.

Even when she looked at the pictures of only he and his wife, she could tell he was happy. Although she denied it to herself, she wanted that too. But her heart was damaged, unable to recognize what real love looked like.

He stood up and yawned, trying hard not to wake Kaleela up. He remembered turning over at some point, not feeling Shona's legs at the other end of the sectional. He could have taken off then, but he wanted to see her one last time before his day got started.

He patted his pockets, looking for his cell. With only the dim light that seeped inside from the sun, he squinted, hoping to see it nearby.

"You're looking for this?" Shona asked him, holding his cell in one hand and a cup of coffee in the other.

Gone was her Hello Kitty onesie, now wearing a pair of black boy shorts and a hot pink tank top. Her hair wrapped up tightly in a black wrap exposed her freshly washed face that was blemish-free.

"Good morning," he said, clearing his throat as he walked towards her. "Still love pink."

"Yup, why not?"

"Looks good on you." To that she said nothing, a pregnant pause in the air when he said, "Thanks."

When he grabbed it, she looked away, almost holding her breath as she fought hard not to look at him before she walked inside of the kitchen. He wasn't expecting much conversation, but he could tell she was in deep thought. Not going too deep, he wanted to make sure they were good before he took off to head home, following her.

Since getting married, he'd never spent a Christmas morning away from his kids and his wife. Even though he didn't mean to stay out all night, he knew he needed to make this visit count.

"And thank you for last night," he said, the hairs on her body standing as soon as she heard his voice. Its raspy texture tugging at her soul.

"No problem," she said, taking slow sips. He could smell the hazelnut coffee brewing, reminding him of home. Myriah was a huge coffee drinker, from a fresh breakfast blend to a dark roast, but it was the hazelnut aroma that did it for him.

"I'm surprised you're up early." He walked up behind her as she placed her cup down on the counter, turning around with a forced smile.

"I couldn't sleep," she whispered, not wanting to look at him but she did. He gently embraced her, placing his chin on the top of her head. She felt good, warm, familiar and like his.

"Sorry 'bout that, ma," he said, releasing her. "I know me coming through unannounced was rude as fuck, but I do appreciate you letting me park for the night in your spot. I sort of needed to clear the air between us. Shit just hasn't felt right since that day. I've been trying to do this for a minute."

She shrugged her shoulders, causing him to hug her even more when he saw she was trying to be tough. He lifted her chin, giving her a soft peck on the lips. When he did, he didn't want to let go, but he had to. He knew Shona. She was loyal to a fault and that fault was him in human form. That only made her be in her feelings as he gave what she'd always gotten, always wanted. She had every right to be mad, but she was tired. She just wanted to stop hurting, letting it all go.

The house was so quiet, but they both could hear the birds chirping just outside the window, creating a calmness they both needed. Chico silently thanked God for rescuing him once again as he felt her relax just a little in his arms. He just needed her to forgive him.

"It's cool," she lied, clipping her responses to avoid saying how she really felt.

"Naw, not really but I want it to be, you know? I need it to be. Shit, we were like best friends, ma. That has to count for something. Maybe we start over being just friends."

She said nothing at first, her stomach churning as if she swallowed something foul. They could never be just friends in her eyes, but the alternative was not having him in her life at all. Sadly, this one night made her remember the good times.

"Mmmm, friends," she said more to herself as she looked down, taking a deep breath.

His cell phone rang, vibrating in his pocket as if God was stepping in to help him get out of there. Without looking, he knew it could only be his wife. *Myriah,* he thought to himself, shooting her a text. He'd never lie to her, telling her he needed to close the door on his past. He could tell the late hours he kept would be a potential argument, but the last thing he would do was lie.

"Guess that means it's time to go." Shona released herself from his embrace, eager to put some space in between them.

"Yeah, it's Myriah," he admitted with ease as he prepared himself to leave. He was glad he didn't have to lie anymore. Lies cost him the last three years. He was interested in their new normal, hoping she was open to it.

"Welp, it was fun." She wasn't trying to be funny, but it did come out that way.

"Hey," he whispered, slowly raising his hand as he gently stroked her cheek with the back of his hand. "You, Shonasia Bradley, are the perfect woman for the right man. The right one who would be crazy to let you go."

"Hmmm," was all she said.

"I'm serious, girl. And you're doing your thing with the shop."

"I'm impressed. So, what don't you know about me?" she asked, chuckling as she rolled her eyes and smiled. "Nosy ass."

Chico laughed. He was very familiar with The Palace. She took money from her cut after leaving The Crew and went straight legal. She never came back, diving right into doing something she naturally did well. That was hair.

Kaleela, still a gangster, helped out around the shop, but Chico knew The Palace was well known all over although Shona kept a low profile.

"Yeah, I know," he admitted, scratching the back of his neck. He had to stop Myriah from checking it out a few times over the years, unsure of how things would turn out once she saw who ran it.

"Like I thought," Shona smirked, then smiled. "Your girl should come sometimes. She's actually quite beautiful, Chico."

"Yeah, she is," he said, feeling his heart swell. "But so are you and for that, I'm sorry. I really am, ma. I never wanted you to feel less than anything when it came to her. She just got me in ways I can't explain.

But guess what? Some nigga is going feel the same about you. I just pray that any harm I've caused over the years, won't stop you from seeing just how fucking amazing you are. It was never you, Shonasia.

Naw, that was all me. I'm the selfish motherfucker, a selfish motherfucker who's in love with his wife," he said, patting his chest. "It was my dick that was fucking shit up and when I saw you, old feelings came back. I just ask that you forgive me and get back out there. You know, with the whole dating thing."

" Oh no, I'm good," Shona said, taking a large gulp of coffee.

She wished it was one of those bottles she'd tossed in the trash, but coffee would have to do. Hearing him confess to being in love with his wife was hard, but necessary she supposed.

"But I do accept your apology. You have a wonderful family, great looking children. You really do. Those kids are beyond gorgeous," she said with a smile. A genuine one, too.

"Oh yeah?" he said, smiling with a smirk on his face. "You've been checking out my kids, huh?"

He knew his wife. She was a selfie queen and the kids fell victim to that. He couldn't walk the streets without someone telling him about a picture they saw of his kids. They were the reason, more than his wife, that he had to walk away and let her go.

"Yes, Chico. I have. Oh, and congratulations on the latest addition to your family. You finally got yourself a junior."

He was born after their encounter in New York. Myriah was pregnant, and neither knew it at the time.

"And he's giving me hell too," he said, laughing as he thought about his youngest. "Well, let me get out of here. She's about to get the kids up. My oldest son knows what's up but to my two younger ones think this fat ass white man brought them some gifts. I kind of got to pretend that he did."

"You know, I wish my father, whoever he is or was, would have been there on any Christmas morning. Shoot, I don't care if he was empty-handed. It still would have been better having him there."

"Yeah, I know," he said, wishing the same for her. "A'ight, shorty. Take care of yourself, a'ight?" he said, wanting to hold her one more time, but knew better.

"I will," she said too quickly, feeling emotional as his arms flinched, struggling not to touch her.

She couldn't believe this was it. They had finally made peace with each other. It still hurt, but the hole she had in her heart had somehow closed. She might even dare to say that it was filled with self-love, but if asked what that was, she couldn't say. All she knew was that she was ready to turn the page and start a new chapter in her life.

He went for it really fast, kissing on her the forehead before he took off, never once looking back.

She prayed neither of them did.

CHAPTER SIX

It was New Year's Eve and like every year, the West family held one of the largest celebrations at the Intercontinental Hotel in downtown Miami. The night was filled with fun with a live band playing anything from Teddy Pendergrass's "Love TKO" to Bruno Mars's "Treasure".

Then, just like any black function, line dancing like the Wobble was a crowd favorite. It was one of the few times X would see his mother looking genuinely happy. She had a knack for putting on parties from catering to decorating. She never charged anyone, often lending a hand simply because she loved it.

X even got a little emotional watching his father and mother. He hadn't seen them appear to be enjoying each other's company like this since he was a kid. They were dancing like they were deeply in love, fooling others because he knew the truth.

His father even dipped her back, catching her and gently kissing her as the room went wild. He hated it was all for show, but seeing his mother smile offered some comfort to him.

"The judge still got it," Ace said to X, sitting down at his table while everyone else mingled. Gator and Tooley, weren't too far away, rarely sitting down. While X and Ace naturally studied the room, Gator and Tooley would take it over from dancing to drinking.

Ace, the dark and handsome one of the group, had jet-black curly hair that blended in with his full beard. A leading detective with the city of Miami, Ace was almost a local celebrity appearing on *The First 48* every week.

If his boys didn't know any better, they thought Ace was getting all his leads by making extra house calls in exchange for information. He wasn't trying to wife anyone, but if she had body and a face and could cook and not gag, Ace was adding her to the line-up.

Gator was the nerd and undercover freak. All the girls in school sought him out to do their homework, but most paid him by sucking him off. He went from being the outcast to that dude really quickly once a few of them let him test them out. Being rather endowed, Gator earned his name because it was said his dick "had a lot of bite".

Being on the tall side, Gator was now a ladies man. His chestnut brown skin complementing his neatly lined goatee that surrounded his full lips. He wasn't buff, but his toned body got him a lot of action. It didn't hurt he was paid, earning more than six figures as a chief financial officer for a large global insurance company.

Tooley, an A&R musical label, was what the women called their best friend. And he was. That worked quite well, especially when he wanted to get close to them. When he did, his shoulder was like a pillow leading to pillow talking and then fucking. His equation was simple and cost him nothing since he refused to pay for pussy.

His only downside was his height. Standing at 5'6", Tooley went for tall women just to prove his only downside was his height. He looked like Hakeem from *Empire*. It didn't hurt he could freestyle, often rapping on sight that wooed most women his way.

They used to laugh, calling him corny, but corny got him three baby mamas, and they were all baddies. His only fault was picking women who had no ambition except having his babies.

In college, while Toley deejayed all the parties, Gator collected the money. In fact, there wasn't a college party they threw that wasn't filled with a gang of women. And they all could get it, from thick to slim. They loved women and the women loved them. Parties were not only a way to maintain their popularity status, but also a way to eat as they got paid to host them.

Ace and X took on the role of security just in case a rival fraternity started making noise or a dude got in his feelings about his bitch gawking at them. Life was good back then and now here they are years later, older but still single. Now X was too, and they were glad, hoping to get back to the days of old.

"Shit, I guess. My dad's something else," X replied, tossing back a glass of that Hardy cognac as he watched his parents behave like a model of marital bliss.

X saw a few victims he wanted to get at, but he played his position tonight watching his sister. She'd been doing well, going to AA meetings and all, but just when they felt Reagan was on the right path, she would relapse.

So tonight at her table, they had a few bottles of sparkling Apple Cider. X watched her pout, but he ignored her, feeling good after his third glass.

Then all of a sudden, a throwback came on. It was Montell Jordan's "This is How We Do it". Immediately, that pout she rocked like makeup was a thing of the past. X, feeling some type of way, watched how she got a lot of attention, half naked in a peach, shimmery bodycon dress that stopped right underneath her ass.

It matched her copper-bronzed, short, texturized hair that was similar to the way Eve wore her hair back in the day. But even on a casual day in some jeans and a tank, Reagan was effortlessly turning heads and X knew it.

He was a man. All the things he'd done to women over the years, made him hot watching his sister shake her ass as she owned the floor. Gator, too, who stood on the side of the dance floor near her table. He told them he did to be close to the bar.

X didn't know all the details, if any honestly, but the times that Gator got missing often lined up once Reagan landed back in town when she was in college. Gator knew how much X loved his sister, but to him, she wasn't a little a girl. She'd somehow gained a spot in his heart and he was stuck, trying to make sense of what to do.

Reagan didn't make that easy, wanting to be a secret. It just seemed she somehow forget that whenever she ran off a woman that Gator was around. X eyed them both suspiciously as she flirted with his boy, winding to the music as Gator imagined his mouth all over her body.

Instead of sampling one of the many women who easily fit into his world called corporate America, Gator fell for his best friend's sister who had him by the balls. He was love sick, and he knew it too.

"You sure Reagan ain't drinking?" Ace asked X, watching her as she swirled her hips in a circle as if someone was grinding on her.

"If she is, someone slipped her something. Every bartender in here already knows she is not to be served. I made sure of that," he told Ace, watching how she motioned for Gator to come on the dance floor.

Like a puppy, he went, smiling every step of the way. His tongue glided across his teeth, enjoying the private dance she gave him although they were in public.

"You know those two got something going on, right?" Ace said to X, watching him stretch his legs out to ease the tension.

X wasn't feeling it, but Reagan was grown and sneaky. If he acted on it knowing his sister, he'd kill one of his best friends because she chose to be a hoe. They watched Gator pull Reagan in close, tugging down on her dress. He subtly kissed her forehead and she smiled, sticking out her tongue.

"Yo, you saw that?" Ace said a little too loud, catching the attention of a few people of the dance floor. "His bitch ass in love." Ace laughed as he stood up, watching Reagan work her magic on him.

"Long as he don't fuck my sister over, he can be whatever he wants to be. But I'll talk to him. He knew Jessica was feeling him."

"Nigga, stop lying. She's feeling you. I know you see her over there mean mugging your ass." X shrugged his shoulders, ignoring her while Tooley hung around near Jessica's table.

X told her once they even went there, she'd have to find a new job. She pushed and pushed, catching him one day with his dick in her mouth. He was close to fucking her on her desk with the door unlocked. That's when he knew she had to go, terminating her a few days later.

Because he knew she needed the work and was good at what she did, X found her a law office up the street. It didn't hurt it was one willing to pay her more money. Still, Jessica wouldn't let go, hitting him up and asking if he wanted to go out for lunch. So her showing up tonight, felt like one more attempt for her to have her way with him. Especially since she didn't work for him anymore.

"Fuck Jessica," X grumbled, his eyes still fixed on Gator and Regan.

"Man, what's that's supposed to mean? Y'all were cool at one point."

"We still are. It's Jessica that be on that bullshit. No different than Avery, playing me close and friendly. Then got mad when I checked her, reminding her I meant what I said. Now imagine if I would have fucked her."

"See, that's where you messed up," Ace replied, grinning as he sat back down and leaned over. "It should be about sex and sex only."

"You're sick," X shot back. "That girl is still young. Too young, actually."

"Not according to the law. Besides, you two are adults."

"And both have to consent. Once I said I'm good, why she was trying to fuck?"

"Word?" he said, laughing at his best friend who admitted to running away from pussy.

"Fuck you. I'm good, Ace. So chill with all of that," X warned him.

Ace laughed, tossing his glass of Hennessey back. He enjoyed getting X all riled up. He hoped his boy would get laid tonight to take off some of that edge he had.

Once they just sat back and chilled, enjoying the scene, they both were feeling good. X had had a rough year, but he was determined to start his new one off right, tossing another his own glass back that was brought his way. He didn't even have to go the bar either, a magic pull that Ace noticed and chuckled about.

Relationships were emotional breeding factors that led to a boatload of poor choices. It's why he really didn't want Reagan dealing with Gator. Not because he didn't trust boy. Relationships just stirred up feelings, feelings that could drive even the most sane person to want to drink.

"Relax, Reagan can handle herself. It's Gator that's in trouble. Look at him," Ace said, pointing their way. X's jawline tightened. "She got him grinning, pinching his cheek. Fuck that, it's him we'll be taking to rehab." Right then, Gator lovingly grabbed her by the chin and slobbed her down.

"Damn!" Ace shouted, clapping his hands. "I told you, boy. And he's hitting that tonight."

"We're really gone sit here and talk about Reagan and who she's giving it up to? That's my sister and he's like a brother. Now, because of that, you better tell him to tread lightly, Ace. I'm doing motherfucking best to stay out of it."

They then heard a few women squeal and laugh a few tables over, waving at Ace and X. Ace nodded his head, holding his glass up. "Now see, that's what we need to get at. Fuck Gator and Reagan for now, with your warden ass."

Now staring at his sister and best friend, although he'd never admit it, he really was jealous. He wanted Gator and Reagan happy, but not having that someone you're intimate with to bring the New Year in with was a first for him in a long time.

"Well, I'm going to get me another drink, bitch. You got that."

"Yeah, bring me back a Henny and Coke."

"A'ight," X said, walking past Gator and Reagan on his way to the bar.

As the music switched to something slower, Gator's hold on her tightened. He didn't see what others saw. Gator saw a woman in need of love, but finding everything but that. Many days before this stint with sobriety, Gator nursed and bathed her, putting her in bed after a drunken night. It was those times she was beyond vulnerable, telling him how abandoned she felt by her father.

He had never betrayed her trust. Not even to X, but he couldn't help it. Gator was madly in love with a stunning and amazing woman that was an alcoholic. Still, he loved her, not really caring now who saw them.

That was until she would remind him they couldn't be together, pushing him away. So, for now, he got a chance to publicly love on her like a little high school boy with his first girlfriend.

"Rey Rey, how are things with your parents? Y'all started the first session yet?" Gator stroked her face, eager to do more but didn't after she let him get that one kiss in. He just wanted her to know that he was into her, even outside of closed doors. For him, it would never be only about sex even though Reagan's pussy made his toes curl.

She sighed, not wanting to talk about it now. She wished she could leave all of that in the past. To her, counseling was just a formality that never worked. She did, however, enjoy groups and meetings, but sitting down with family and talking about her feelings was out.

To her, Gator was more than enough. She was addicted to him and his dick. She tugged his chin, getting up on her tippy toes to kiss him. She was being extra, watching X in her peripheral vision. That was that rebellious side of her that made her feel alive. With no hesitation, Gator entertained her, gently gripping her ass as he lifted her up just a little.

She then caught Jessica staring their way. From what she knew, Jessica had a thing for X, but she'd kill her if she thought Gator was up for grabs. She knew women like Jessica didn't play fair, so neither would she.

"Mmmm," Gator moaned in her mouth. "You better stop it."

"No, you better not," she warned him, her mouth still on his. If Gator could, he would have taken her right there in the middle of the dance floor, but the look on her brother's face along with her dad's was uncomfortable as he looked around.

He quickly put some space in between them, watching X head their way. "Where are you going?" she asked him, giggling. "Too late to run now," she told Gator, rubbing his thick, bushy eyebrows with the pad of her thumb. "I love these. I love everything about you." Gator was hairy, but what she loved the most were his eyebrows that complemented his slanted, dark brown eyes.

"Enough to settle down?" he asked, only to feel her tense up.

"Gator, my sweet, sweet baby. Let's not go there tonight, okay?" she begged just above a whisper. "It's New Year's Eve. I just want you inside of me, fucking me, holding me." That was her way of putting a period at the end of a sentence, shutting him down. "Besides, who else you got but me? Why are you rushing?"

Gator smiled, shaking his head. He couldn't believe X's baby sister had him wide open like this, but she did. He saw her point, but fighting other women off was starting to make others question how he moved if he couldn't produce a woman. He knew after tonight, there would be questions, but he figured he could blame it on the alcohol. Well, for his behavior at least.

"No rush, Rey Rey. No rush at all." He could stay there all night, but Reagan wasn't playing fair, cuffing his dick as their bodies were mashed tightly against each other.

"How about we go to the bathroom," she whispered, feeling his hardness become harder in her hand.

"So I can fuck your legs wobbly, making these people thinking I got you drunk? Hell naw. But I am sticking dick to you when we get out of here. Fuck that," he told her as she continued to massage his muscle.

"Fine, but I'm tired of chasing the dick," she said, faking like she was mad as they swayed to the music. Gator looked down at her, biting his lip. In his heart, he was already chasing her and she knew it. Still, she was prepared for the lectures from others. She just wanted Gator and to have lots of fun.

While Gator and Reagan got lost in each other, Jessica sat alone nursing a glass of wine. She liked Reagan and thought she was hilarious, but to her, she was all about Reagan.

Most days in the office or whenever they were around each other, they got along perfectly. But in many ways, Jessica felt she was just like Avery. X had two women in his life that took more than they gave and Jessica hated that. Now one of them had Gator too.

"You're good over here?" Tooley asked her, taking a seat. Jessica was fuming, watching X ignore her and Gator who was all into a drunk bound to be puking by morning. All night, X laughed in one spot, not even coming over to speak, while Gator acted like she never tried to come on to him.

It was a week after X had let her go. It was one day while on lunch when she ran into Gator. Still in her feeling some type of way about X, she asked Gator to have drink after work with her. Even gave him her number, but he ran like his ass was on fire, not even trying to pretend like he wasn't interested.

Now here was the real whore of the group planting his ass next to her. As soon as Tooley did, it was then that she saw X heading their way.

"Do I look like I'm not good?" she asked Tooley, trying to get him to leave.

Tooley leaned over, staring at her thick, caramel thighs that clung to the gold, fitted dress that almost melted against her skin. Her hair, swooped up high at the top of her head, showed off her neck. Tooley wanted to bite it, having her scream out his name. He didn't give two shits about her being standoffish. He wanted to fuck.

"You look like your pussy is starving for some attention. Face all balled up, body tight. Let me handle that for you," he said casually, like it was appropriate.

"Wait, what?" she squawked, leaning back in disgust.

"Girl, stop it. You know you heard me," he replied, casually taking a sip from his glass. "Let me attend to that pussy for you. See, you've been hollering at the wrong one all this time.

"Says who? Your *three* baby mamas?" she asked, shaking her head.

Tooley laughed, watching Jessica eye fuck X as he got closer to their table. "Yo, that was some mean shit to say. And here I was trying to have coach put me in the game since the ones on the court ain't playing with you."

"And that's some weak shit to say," she shot back, trying to avoid looking directly at X as he got closer. But as quickly as he did, he kept right on going, deflating any hope she had that they would link up. Tooley peeped how her body language changed, tensing up even more, then slumping down as X walked by.

He grabbed his bottle of Grey Goose and stood up. Then he leaned over and pulled her hair out of her face. At first she jumped, then stopped once she realized what he was doing. "There, that's better. You know I got two girls, so doing hair is our thing whenever they come over."

Jessica smiled slightly embarrassed, then dropped her head. She now felt bad for going off on him. "That's cute. And thank you."

"No thanks needed. Listen, never lose sight of who's in front of you, while checking for the one who's not. Trust me, I got three baby mamas for a reason. It's because they all pretend they're still not sharing me. Why? Aye, because they let me." He left after that not even waiting for a response as he left her to her thoughts.

Jessica wasn't sure why he felt the need to tell her that, but it did get her attention. She looked back at X talking and smiling with a female attorney that was just hired at the office she was now working at.

"I don't belong here," she finally said to herself.

She picked up her purse and quickly got up, taking off to run outside to breathe. Tooley watched her as he sat down next to Ace. The asshole in him wanted to follow her, but the man who was raising two girls let her go.

"You see Reagan and Gator?" he asked, switching his attention to something else.

"Yup and don't start X up again when he get back," Ace told Tooley. "He's already tripping."

The woman were into some swinging shit, but Ace knew enough about that to know he wanted to fuck privately. It took him no time to bid them a good night, his eyes dancing around the room in his quest for the next victim.

X had made a few rounds, greeting a few associates, before he headed back their way. He looked over once more and there was Gator, fully committed to publicizing their arrangement. Ace gave Tooley the look that said "shut the fuck up". Surprisingly, he did while Gator looked down lovingly at Reagan, wishing he could speed time up.

The music was now more upbeat, but they continued to sway back and forth. He could feel her heartbeat, her breathing picking up. She didn't like how he controlled even the smallest thing like the air she breathed but he did, even if he didn't know it. That alone scared the shit out her, making it all sexual which was her comfort zone.

Tensing up, Gator was sure after tonight, she would get missing, but he would still be right there whenever she came back. He knew she loved him and since love was patient, he knew waiting was his only choice.

"You saw Jessica and Tooley over there? Now you know that girl does not want him. I honestly think she and X got a little something," Reagan said as he spent her around basking in her beauty. He still had his hand firmly on her backside, shielding her from exposure.

"Don't worry about them. Worry about this fucking dress you're not wearing after tonight," Gator told her, spinning her once more.

"Whatever you say, Garvin," she replied, calling him by his real name. Deciding her statement didn't require an answer, he continued to dance, holding her as the background in the room faded out.

Just then, a woman walked in, looking around that had caught Ace's attention. She seemed to have come alone, or was waiting for someone. Either way, Ace made up his mind he was going to meet her before the night was over. "About time some damn body came in that's looking like a snack I wanna eat."

Tooley sat up, looking around. "Man, where? All these hoes can get it. How you pick out just one? I'm still trying to narrow mine down."

"Ole Jessica ain't bite, huh?" Ace whispered, shooting his eyes at X.

"Damn that," Tooley said, waving him off. "If I wanted to, that would be a wrap. Fuck you think," he said, sucking his teeth. None of them were ever at odds about a bitch and they wouldn't start now. He wasn't hiding from X, so he knew X could have checked him when he saw him over there anyway. "Too much pussy in here just to set your sights only on one."

"Yeah, whatever. And her right there," Ace said, grinning as he pointed her out. She was speaking to one of the staff, clearly looking for her table. "Damn," he said lowly, looking exactly like his type.

"Yeah, that's your type," both X and Tooley said, laughing in response. She even caught their attention, her thick hips working the room as she was escorted to her assigned table.

"Bruh, I ain't got no type," he lied, never wanting to admit any type of woman could lock him down. "If she got a vagina, have all her teeth and can hold a conversation while I'm blowing her back out, she's my type." Ace was joking around, but this mystery woman could definitely get the business. And she was a lady, too. He could tell.

When he saw her, he immediately thought of his mother, may God rest her soul, and his aunt Sarah. They both were quite the beauties, full-figured and all. Anytime his aunt talked about his mother, she always told him how all the men flocked to her no matter her size.

She was always well put together, often described as having a "Coca Cola" body times two. She had plenty of breast, hips and thighs but the flattest stomach. She wore her hair in big curls accentuating her big, dark brown eyes and round, baby-like face.

Even at Aunt Sarah's age, while she was married to the Lord, it never failed whenever Ace visited her home, a different deacon was there eating a plate of food or running an errand for her.

To him, full figured women had the touch that made a man do all kinds of things. Because of his respect for his aunt and love for his mother, he would always have a soft spot in his heart for a big, beautiful woman, although he'd never say it out loud.

"Well, you go handle that. I'm about to see what's up with some food. This shit is whack, honestly. Tooley, you coming?" X wasn't hungry, but watching Ace get some action wasn't for him. He didn't miss Avery, but tonight just wasn't the same and it was starting to get to him.

"Yeah, man. You think I should leave my bottle or take it with me?"

"Nigga, how much money you make?" X asked Tooley, smirking. "Stop having all them damn kids and you won't even care about leaving this damn bottle."

"Whatever," he said, taking his bottle with him. His kids, Pumpkin, JJ and Crayola were his heart, but he easily spent ten grand a month on child support.

Ace walked off, looking hard as shit in his tuxedo. It was a cream-colored tuxedo, making his smooth dark brown skin make most of the women squirm when they looked his way.

Before Ace went to her table, he stopped by the bar and slipped the bartender a twenty-dollar bill for a bottle of Roscato. He wanted to take a glass, but most women would refuse it since they weren't there to watch the bartender make it.

Slowly sliding up to her, Ace cleared his throat getting her attention.

"Oh, shoot! You scared me," she said, holding her chest. A chest he wanted to stick his face in. If he thought she was beautiful from across the room, he was sadly mistaken now. In fact, there were no words what he saw when he looked at her.

Ironically, she wore a cream-colored dress that dipped just a little in the back but fit snuggly around her neck like a choker. He noticed her large breasts sat up nicely as his eyes traveled down to her rather voluptuous thighs and legs. She was easily a size sixteen, but he was ready to toss all of that in his face.

Her makeup wasn't too heavy but it was just enough to highlight the goldish speckles in her eyes. Then the nude, glittered lip gloss made him bite his own lips, imagining them on top of his. He was so caught up with how she looked, he had forgot to even speak.

"Are you okay?" she asked him, leaning back as she looked up at him.

"Who me?" he said, chuckling from embarrassment. "Actually, hell naw, I'm not."

He wanted to be on his best behavior, starting formally, but with a woman as fine as her, he didn't want to waste a second on bullshit, placing the wine down on the table.

"Are you looking for your assigned table? Maybe you should go and ask one of the staff. We can go find one if that helps," she told him, then stopped herself before she said too much.

"We, as in you and your girlfriends?"

"No, we as in me and her," the man replied, standing almost in between them. Ace backed up with a scowl on his face as the man subtly nudged him.

He had no problem backing up and offering an apology, but he couldn't stand an insecure man throwing his weight around because he had a fine bitch on his arm. From the looks of it, she was spooked like she'd been caught stealing candy out of the store. Ace looked at him flexing his jaw with one hand over the other, like he was ready to do something.

"A'ight, but watch your fucking arm. I'm not with that tootie fruity shit. I fuck bitches for fun. Not men."

The mystery woman's face was flushed as she covered her mouth, her eyes wide open. He could tell she'd never heard a man speak to the man she was with like that, but he didn't give no fucks. He wasn't drunk but respect was due no matter who you were, and he could tell this man was a pussy.

"Come again," the man said, bending down as he mean mugged the woman. She looked away, slowly shaking her head in her efforts to avoid eye contact with Ace.

That alone made Ace radar go off. He was ready to kick some ass then. And like X, they both were known for fucking shit up when things got rowdy. Whenever X did visit one of his aunts in the hood, it wouldn't be long before he and Ace were on the court or in the street fighting.

They all took X for a stuck up, rich kid but that soon ended when he proved his money had nothing to do with his hands. And what they didn't learn by fighting in the neighborhood, X's uncle Pookey taught them right after X's eye took a hit that sent him to the ER.

After that, against his mother's wishes, Uncle Pookey picked up him and Ace and every weekend and took them to the gym. To say both had deadly hands was, in fact, an understatement.

"I suggest you back the fuck up," Ace told him as he stood. When he didn't, Ace pushed the man back just enough without him toppling over the woman. "I was just speaking. No harm intended. I couldn't find my table, so she was helping me out."

Ace knew the man didn't believe him, but fighting over a woman that wasn't his wasn't the move. Plus, she already looked terrified. He wasn't about to be the reason she needed to be any more than she already was.

The man stood up straight and smiled, tugging on his tuxedo jacket as he looked down at his date. She immediately looked down, fumbling with her fingers.

Fucking asshole, Ace thought, watching him intimidate a woman he now wished was his, at least for the night. Then he could have a reason to fuck dude up.

"I'm glad she could be of help. Baby, tell—" her date said and paused, looking from her to him. "Excuse me, what's your name?" He grinned when he did, sizing Ace up.

"Doesn't matter," Ace shot back, ready to fuck him up. "You have a very beautiful woman there. She's respectful, too. Nothing but a lady. I like that," he told him, walking around to grab her hand.

She jumped when he touched it, but didn't pull away before Ace kissed the back of her hand. His lips soft, melting her skin upon touch had her warm as she cleared her throat.

He chuckled, but then whispered, "The name is Ace. Detective Ace Alexander. Please remember that." She caught the hint as her hand began to shake. That was a warning he had connections she assumed, hoping both men behaved.

Before Ace could stand up and walk away, he felt a blunt hit to the back of his head, then one on his back. The woman screamed, asking for help while her date slammed his chair down on top of Ace.

The music stopped at the sound of her plea, everyone started screaming and looking around for anyone to intervene. Gator was the closest, taking off to help his boy. Before he could, Ace snatched the man by the ankle, bringing him down to the floor on his back.

"You fucking pussy!" he growled, head butting him twice before he lifted him by his throat, delivering three right blows to his face, cracking his jaw.

While the woman continued to scream for them to stop, he watched the man laugh hysterically before he hocked and spit in Ace's face. Ace hit him again, before Gator and X came and pulled him off him.

His female companion was a mess as she dropped to the floor, crying over him. He mushed her in the face, knocking her on her ass.

"Ah!" she cried out, her head hitting the floor.

"Fuck that," Gator said, hating for a man to put his hands on a woman.

He started kicking him in the face and chest, watching the man laugh each time his foot landed. Tooley, not one to miss out on the action, pulled Gator back before getting in a few stomps to his face. The man could barely see or breathe, his eyes swelling up as his mouth filled with blood.

"We got to get the hell up out of here! Let's go!" X screamed, before kicking the man once in his side, cracking his ribs. Before Ace followed him out, he stopped and apologized to the women over and over. She refused to listen, lying there and crying as she propped herself up on her knees by the man's side.

"Fuck them. Let's get out of here!" Reagan screamed, grabbing Gator by the hand. Before the cops got there, all five of them were in Gator's Escalade truck heading south on I-95. It was almost like old times except for Reagan who was all over Gator, babying him like he'd gotten hit.

Ace wasn't worried, making one call. Even if a guest did give a description or offer up names, that testimony would be discarded of, never making it in the final police report.

"Bruh," Gator said, laughing. "She's staying with me. I got her. You're telling me you don't trust me?" he asked X, lifting his right brow when they headed to his place next with her still in the truck.

After they'd both made it obvious he and Reagan were dealing with each other, he figured why not let that shit all out. They were boys, so he would deal with X later.

"Shit, have I ever said that? Besides, Reagan's grown. I can't regulate what she does, nor how I fuck you up if I have to. You feel me?" he said.

The energy was already tense as they drove through the city, each being dropped off one by one. The fiends were out tonight, walking all up and down the street as the fireworks went off. When Gator was headed to X's spot first instead of his parents to drop Reagan off next, X stopped him.

"Whatever," he said, smiling as he shook his head. Reagan quickly grabbed his hand, squeezing to get his attention. Her warm brown eyes said it all, forcing him to relax.

"Gator, Reagan may run your ass, but not me."

"X, please," she whispered, feeling emotional.

"Man, I still can't believe y'all been getting over on me," X said more to himself, watching them as she latched on to Gator's arm.

"It's not his fault," Reagan interjected. "It was all me, X. Please don't blame him."

"Hey, I spoke on it. He heard me, so I'm good."

"Thanks, man. I love her," he said, looking down at Reagan like she was a bag of sweets. It's why he called her sweetness. She stretched her eyes, shocked he said that out loud in front of her brother, but she loved him, too.

X shook his head at them. He decided after his fuck up with women, maybe minding his business was best.

"Love y'all dumb asses, too."

CHAPTER SEVEN

Two months later

It was four o'clock in the morning and Shona jumped up, hearing her cell phone ring. She usually put it on vibrate, but whenever Kaleela went out, she didn't just in case she needed her.

She snatched it off her dresser and saw an unfamiliar number. "Hello," she said, clearing her throat as she rubbed her eyes.

"Yes, this is Detective Alexander. Is this Shonasia Bradley?" Shona shot up straight in her bedroom, wondering why the laws would be on her line.

In all of her years of trapping, the only ones she ever spoke to were on their payroll. Even then, unless they spoke on burners, she still didn't speak to them.

She got up and quickly walked down the hall to see if Kaleela was home. She flipped on the light, seeing an empty bed.

"Uh, yeah. This is she."

"Ms. Bradley, I have a Kaleela Bradley here with me—"

"Why? What happened? Is she okay?" she asked in a panic, looking around to slip anything that resembled shoes on her feet. She found her hot pink Nike slides but couldn't find her keys. "Damn," she cursed, crawling on the floor to see if they fell under or behind her bed.

"Officially, yes. Unofficially, not really," he said. She heard his voice muffled, talking to someone in the background.

"Sir! Excuse me!" she yelled into the phone. "Hello, are you talking to me? What the hell does that even mean?"

She closed her bedroom door, finding her keys behind it. The only person that could have done that was Kaleela. She was always hiding stuff just to aggravate her.

"One minute," he said, resuming his conversation. She could hear ruffling and movement, then her sister's voice. "I'm back. Meaning, no she's not under arrest but she should be. She got a mouth on her too." Shona groaned, praying Kaleela would just shut up until she got to wherever they were.

"Look, text me the address and I'm coming. I'm so sorry, Officer Mister Detective."

Ace laughed, never hearing anyone call him all three at the same time. He wasn't even on duty. After a night of pool, they headed to The Lion's Den. A strip club that Kaleela sometimes frequented trying to pick up some new action. Her usual spot, King of Diamonds, was no longer in business. It had been shut down as the owner allowed it to go into foreclosure.

When she only wanted a few drinks, some chicken wings, and a lap dance, King of Diamonds was her spot. But now that they were closed, only Tootsie's had good food on the north end. Unfortunately, Tooties was full of white bitches. She wasn't fucking with them. No, Kaleela loved her some black pussy, choosing to take a ride in the deep south part of Miami

"The Lion's Den? You mean all the way down by Florida City?" she barked, mad she had to drive all the way down there.

"That's the one," he said. "I could bring her home, but like I said, this is unofficial. Once I put her in a vehicle with me and something happens, that's on me. And let's be honest, shorty is wild."

"Tell me about it," she mumbled, locking her front door as she hopped in her truck. She'd just gotten a Range Rover for the New Year as a gift to herself right after Christmas.

She hadn't even broken it in, and now she had to ride at least fifty miles to and from to get her sister.

"Well, I'm coming, but let me warn you that I'm on the north end. Give her a bottle of water and pop her ass in the mouth, because I swear you might have to arrest me if she says one damn thing to me. No, make that two bottles of water. Her ass is professional drinker."

"Already did. Right now she even tried to get out of her wheelchair. Can she even walk?"

"Well, you have my permission to body slam her ass on her back until I get there."

Ace didn't respond. He could tell she was frustrated. It was four of them and one of them could easily follow her back but he'd done more than he would normally do being off duty. All he wanted was for her to get home safely. He could tell from what she was pushing, she came from money, and not the legal kind.

While they waited, Gator stood in front of the strip club fussing with Reagan. She'd been dodging him all week, not taking his calls. He tricked her, calling her from a Google number and she messed around and picked it up.

"That's what I got to do to get you to answer your phone, Rey Rey?"

Reagan sighed, sitting up and barely awake. She found out last week she was pregnant and she didn't want to have it. She loved Gator, but she was still young and was unsure what being a parent was even like. To her, life had just started, her being twenty-five while Gator was a bit older at thirty-one.

"Gator, what time is it?"

"Time for you to stop acting like some little ass girl. It's been a week, Rey Rey. A whole fucking week. If it wasn't for X, I wouldn't have known if you were dead or alive. And I heard you stopped going to your meetings. What's up with that shit?"

"Ugh," she grunted, hating she just couldn't be who he needed her to be.

Being with him required her to be accountable and consistent. She struggled with that, loving to party and have fun. Fun sometimes even included random sex with random faces. It made her feel alive and free.

She did, however, love how he made her feel, but he was starting to sound more and more like her father. Anyone that reminded her of him, she ran from.

"Rey Rey? Talk, baby girl," he warned her, feeling himself get weak for her even though it was him that should be mad. "I'm trying to check in with you, sweetness. Tell me what's up."

He hated her little outbursts that failed to communicate anything of value. Hearing the compassion coupled with pain in his voice was overwhelming for her. She preferred having temper tantrums. It was better than talking about her feelings. She didn't want therapy. She wanted to fuck.

"Gator, I'm not a little girl. I don't need to tell you every single detail of my life, where I go, who I go with, who I fuck, who—"

He laughed. "Oh, so we're fucking other people now, Rey Rey? I can't believe this shit," he said to himself, feeling the rage course through his body.

"Garvin—"

"Now, I'm Garvin?" he asked her, ready to strangle her fucking neck. She was trying to be funny. "Okay, I see. Listen, I get it. Hey, if it's not my dick, it's someone else's. I don't even know why I am even fucking surprised," he huffed, wishing she was in front of him right now.

"Bitch, what?" she scoffed.

"Yeah, like I said," he laughed, disgusted with her. "I knew you couldn't handle being with a man like me. Shit, I even lied to myself, hoping you could at least fake it. Just know when you see me and I'm with the next bitch, it was you that pushed me that way."

"And I will fuck you up," she growled, rubbing her stomach. She wanted to throw up, imagining him fucking another bitch.

"Why? Because I want a wife, babies, a bitch to go on vacations with? Now out of respect for X, I'll say this nicely. Grow the fuck up and dead my fucking number," he told her before he hung up in her face.

"No, you grow the fuck up! I don't need you or anyone!" she screamed to no one, feeling a knot in her stomach.

She not only wanted to call back, but she needed to. She tried, pressing his name from the call log, but it went straight to voicemail. After three more tries, she knew she he'd blocked her calls.

She couldn't tell him she was pregnant, afraid her drinking might have hurt the baby. She also knew she wasn't ready and he deserved better. He deserved that wife and kids on a family vacation.

"Well, little one. Just know Mommy loves you, but even you deserve better than me," she whimpered, wiping her eyes as she tried to see.

She went on the internet, searching for a list of abortion clinics. Once she found one, she dialed it. It rang repeatedly, unfortunately going unanswered. Feeling like shit, she reached over to her nightstand and grabbed a large bottle of tequila.

Tequila had become her comforter, feeling a calmness flood her body and mind. It burned going down, but it actually felt good to her once it settled.

"Yep, this is what I need. You are always there for me," she said to herself, now giggling. After tossing her head back emptying the bottle, she tossed it against the wall, breaking it.

Bam!

She fell back in the bed and covered her face, crying herself to sleep.

CHAPTER EIGHT

After Tyson spent a few weeks in the hospital, he had been home for almost a month now. Gabby, although feeling guilty, wasn't looking forward to it. Each day she came home not finding him there was like a dream come true.

She loved her fiancé but no matter what she did, she somehow always angered him. She knew if he hadn't been hauled off to the hospital, it would have been her going instead of him.

For the past seven years, Tyson had been all she'd ever known. After meeting in college, the jock somehow fell for the quirky, fat, and cute nerd. Falling in love, he made her make him a promise one night that she has lived to regret. There wasn't a day that had gone by that she didn't remember it.

It was the first week of finals. The frenzy from all night study sessions and surviving off snacks instead of food was at an all-time high on campus. Gabby, who seemed to ace all of her finals, was now studying with Tyson. He was sent to her after being at a point of flunking out by his coach.

He was already on probation for financial aid with the threat of being kicked out. His dream of going pro to play ball was over. He had the talent, but a bad attitude. So all he had going in his favor was to finish up strong academically and get a degree.

After years of barely getting by, he actually had to care now and it was down to the wire. If he got one C, that was it for him. His coach told him he might be able to help him find a local coaching job, but that required a degree, too.

While he was witty and charming, often winning people over, his wit and charm couldn't get win him a passing grade. His only hope was this frumpy chick sitting in front of him who was afraid to even look him in the eyes.

He was terrified of anyone seeing the two of them, but after the first two days, he settled down. She seemed cool, plus she took her time with him. She never made him feel stupid, always praising him when he got something right. By the end of the week, he felt like he'd known her all of his life.

She went from being the frumpy and chubby girl, to a girl who was cute when you really looked beyond her size and wiry eyeglasses. One day, after getting cursed out by his father, he failed to show up for his last day of tutoring.

Unlike other girls, Gabby actually cared, getting worried. After stopping by his room and being laughed at by his roommates, she scurried off to her dorm room and cried. She had a crush on him, often looking forward to the time they had spent together.

She knew they weren't dating, but it was the way he looked at her when he smiled, making her feel as if she was the only one he could see. She even knew he had a father that ruled by an iron fist. One call from him would leave Tyson almost paralyzed, especially when he chose college over the family's carpet business.

His mother had a heart attack recently and her prognosis wasn't good. According to his sister Tammy, money was tight which made it even harder not going to the pros. So, it was all or nothing, putting his faith in Gabby.

"Hey, where have you been?" she asked him, after he was let in by her roommate entering her room. "We were supposed to meet at one on the second floor in the student cafe."

Tyson, not even acknowledging her question, lied on her bed and stared at the ceiling. She was at her desk, going over her notes feeling like a real lame. Somehow, that made her feel close to him.

He'd only been there once, remembering the sugary cotton candy smell he smelled even now. It was her lotion. He never asked, but he saw it that one time he came. He looked forward to smelling it, often getting upset whenever she didn't wear it.

He stared at her, but said nothing. He felt overwhelmed and ashamed that he didn't have the one person he trusted to tell how he was feeling. Gabby quickly gauged something was off, sitting on the edge of the bed next to him.

"Hey, what's wrong?" His furrowed brows told her he was thinking and whatever it was, couldn't be good.

She gently placed her hand on his shoulder and he flinched. In his family, they only touched when it was time to be disciplined. An occasional hug during the holiday was somewhat normal, but touching for no reason other than to hit was foreign to him.

Then he started hyperventilating, sitting up as he tried to breathe. Gabby was at a loss, unsure of what to do. She got up to go and get help, but he stopped her, catching her off guard.

"No, don't!" he said, panicking. "I'm fine!"

"Sorry," she mumbled, feeling scared. His eyes were wild and he now had sat up with his legs on the side of the bed, taking slow and deep breaths.

"I am," he said, taking one final deep breath slowly as he looked at her. "But what if I'm not, are going to leave me? What, you're disappointed because I didn't show up for that stupid session?" All of a sudden, his anger and anxiety was directed at her. She was so confused, unsure if she should run. "Huh, Gabby? Tell me," he demanded lowly, grabbing her hand.

"I—I'm—"

"I'm sorry. I'm sorry," he said, realizing what he had done when he let her go He then clenched his fists, his eyes following as he fought back the tears.

"Uh—"

"It's okay. You don't have to accept my apology. You want to know why, Gabby?" he asked, his eyes filled with remorse. His tone, too. "Because I'm going to fail. So save yourself some time. That's what I do. I fucking fail."

"But you were doing so well," she croaked, rubbing both of her arms. He could tell he had spooked her, hating he was such a fuck up to a person that had been so kind to him.

"Come here," he demanded but this time softer, reaching his hand out towards her. He didn't know how to be gentle, but he was definitely trying.

She shook her head no. He sighed, dropping his head, then he asked her again. "Look, I'm sorry I told you. Please, don't make me beg."

When she didn't move, he stood up and walked towards her. Once he reached her, she surprisingly didn't reject his touch when he grabbed both of her hands. They were soft as he rubbed the inside with the pad of his thumbs.

"So, are you trying to leave me?" he whispered this time in her ear, moving her wild, curly hair away from her face and neck. He inhaled the scent, drawing him to taste her warm, flushed skin. "Fuck, Gabby. I love the way you smell."

"Ah—ah, thank you," she stuttered, as he walked backwards still holding her hands. He stopped as they go tot her bed. Their eyes locked in, he saw uncertainty in hers, but he knew what he felt. He wanted her, patting his lap once he sat down.

"No, I—I might hurt you." He laughed. Gabby was indeed a big girl but Tyson wasn't by far a small guy. He was 6'1", weighing at least two hundred and twenty pounds. He was bulky, but toned.

"Girl, you can't hurt me," he told her then laughed once more as she sat down. "I'm a big nigga." He bit his lip, staring at hers. They looked soft. He wanted to feel them, running his thumb across her bottom lip. "Can I kiss you?" he asked.

She nodded her head yes, feeling all giddy inside. She'd never been kissed before, wanting to record all of it in her mind. It may have sounded silly to some, but she had never imagined a guy wanting to kiss her. Especially not a guy as fine and handsome as Tyson.

"Wait, is it okay if I keep my eyes open?" she asked, feeling embarrassed after she did.

"Shorty, that's on you," he whispered, leaning in. She braced herself staring at his mouth. His lips, soft and full, landed just below her ear, causing goose bumps. She was waiting for him to kiss her mouth, but that alone sent chills down her spine. She gasped and jumped. "Yo, you funny. Gabby, I haven't even kissed you yet."

"Okay," she whispered, dropping her head. She knew how inexperienced she was, praying he didn't change his mind. That alone gave him a hard-on.

Tired of talking, he grabbed the back of neck, bringing her face down to his. Her soft, henna brown eyes with golden specks stretched in anticipation. In that moment, he felt strong watching her yield to him. It was the most powerful feeling he had ever felt.

The only thing that would make it better was feeling that feeling forever. After gently kissing her mouth, he traveled up and kissed her forehead, scratching and massaging her scalp.

She moaned, closing her eyes, and he smiled. "Open your eyes."

Immediately, she did, doing as she was told. He smiled again. To him, the eyes never lied but usually whenever he looked in his father's, he saw hate. With her, he saw something else. It was love.

"You ever lied to me, you know with all those compliments?" he asked, staring at her eyes as he waited to see if he saw something different.

"No, I've never," she said quickly.

"Never?" he asked, wanting her to say it again.

"No, never," she replied, almost pleading for him to believe her.

"Would you ever leave me?" he asked, unsure if she understand enough to respond, but she did anyway.

"No, Tyson. I could never, ever leave you."

He caught her face in both hands and delicately kissed her lips. Hers were stiff at first, unsure of where this was going as his gripped tightened. The kiss grew hungry as he pulled her down on top of him as he leaned back. She then felt a tingling sensation between her legs, something she had never felt before.

The deeper the kiss, the harder he became underneath her. He gripped her from behind, rubbing her ass. Then he rolled them over, placing her underneath him, kissing her more passionately. She was soft and she felt good.

"Tyson," she moaned in his mouth as his right hand cupped one breast. As he assaulted her mouth, softly biting and pulling on her bottom lip, he slipped his hand underneath her shirt. Her skin was hot, hot for him, and he wanted to feel all of it.

He stopped kissing her, pulling her shirt up just enough to expose her breasts covered in a soft pink bra. He smiled thinking of the color of cotton candy. He briefly stopped, checking to see if she maybe had changed her mind. She looked scared, but not of him. Right then, he knew it was her first time.

Still, watching her chew on her bottom lip told him all he needed to know. He quickly pulled off her top and freed her breasts, her huge, chocolate areolas hardening for him. He touched one, watching it draw up. Because of her size, she often wore leggings that adjusted with her size.

Although she was considered the "big girl," watching her in those often bothered him. He could easily see all of her curves, even from walking. After today, she wasn't wearing another pair if he had a say in it.

He sat then sat up on his knees between her legs, lifting one leg at a time to slide them off. Her pink panties, while not considered sexy, matched her bra. He *smiled at that, too. But what excited him the most was the scent from her untouched pussy.*

"Look at me, keep your eyes on me," he instructed her, slipping the seat of her panties to the side. When he did, he made her lie down as he positioned his mouth between her juicy, good smelling ass thighs.

Her mouth opened, feeling her nerves unravel as he flicked and caressed her hooded mound with his tongue. The slickness quickly appeared, coating his lips. She arched her back, opening up herself to him.

He continued to deliver soft sucks as he lifted one leg and rested it on his shoulder. Her juices ran down his mouth as he lifted the other leg, resting it on his shoulder.

Tyson sucked and licked, and licked and sucked until Gabby couldn't take it anymore. He sat up, pushing her legs against her shoulders and dove inside of her with his thick length, stretching her to capacity.

Gabby's eyes widened when he did. He shuddered, feeling her tight walls grip his dick. Gabby, siting up on her elbows, winced from the pain. Then instinctively as he issued soft, yet firm strokes, she began to grind her pussy against him, wanting even more of him.

"That's it, baby. Feed me this pussy, this good ass pussy."

Gabby wound her hips as he guided them, watching his eyes now softened as he dropped his head back. Unlike earlier, he was now feeling out of control.

"Mmmhmm," he moaned, trying to stop himself from exploding. It was too soon. He wanted more, he needed more. So he pulled out and lifted her ass, lodging his tongue inside of her.

"Ah, ah, ah," she groaned. "Oohh, ah, ahhhh."

"That's it. That's it," he said, his mouth full of her pussy and ass.. "Give it all to me, fuck." He then covered her entire pussy with his whole mouth, siphoning all of her juices.

"Ahhhhhhh, ba—by. Uh, pleaseeeee," she cried out.

"Uh huh," he replied, shaking his head no. "Not—not until you promise me again." His voice, deep and husky, rattled against her core. He snatched his mouth away, getting her attention.

"What—what are—" she started to say until he cut her off.

"Promise that you will never leave me," he demanded, his voice steady and low.

"I—I promise! Baby, I swear. I—I promise," she stammered.

"Yes," he hissed, easing his massive dick back inside. She involuntary sat up and he caught her mouth. "That's it," he growled, spraying her insides with his seed.

After several hours of discovering what made her release from one position to the next, sunset found them all spent and tangled up in each other's arms. While Tyson thought she was knocked out, Gabby heard him speak words she could still hear today.

"You are mine. You will always be mine. There is nothing and no one that can ever take you away from me. I'd die first, Gabby."

Without prompting, she said, "I promise to never, ever leave you."

His mother died a few days later and so did his soul. He never returned home, blaming his father for the early death of his mother.

Gabby took a deep breath, remembering how it all began. She looked around almost happy until she remembered she wasn't home alone. She was looking forward to a quiet evening coupled with a nice foot soak as she stood up, taking deep breaths.

That all ended when she picked up her cell and saw five missed calls and six text messages. She had placed it on the charger as soon as she got in her truck, forgetting about it. It was him.

She felt her chest tightening once she stepped out. "No, you can do this, Gabby. He needs you. Who else does he have? Just give it some time. He will finally see you are in his corner," she said to herself.

That was the little pep talk she gave herself every day. She'd gotten sidetracked, deep in her thoughts, missing their neighbor, Mr. Morgan, as he walked up to her.

"Oh God!" she yelped, grabbing her chest. "Mr. Morgan, you scared me." She laughed nervously, fanning her face.

"Sorry about that Miss Gabby," he softly said and smiled. "I'm about to crank up the mower and cut my yard. Sun's going down. You need me to hit yours right quick?"

Gabby dropped her head in shame. Usually that was Tyson's department. Most times, he would pay a lawn service to come in, but lately all he did was mope around. She figured why not since he was out there anyway, but only if she paid him.

"Uh, sure. You know Tyson's still recovering. I'm not sure how much he usually pays our guy, but let me write you a check." She reached in her purse, pulling out her checkbook. By the time she pulled out a pen and turned around to ask for the amount, Mr. Morgan was gone.

"Mr. Morgan!" she yelled, and he shook his head no.

"It's on me! Besides, my wife would kill me if I charged you. You look tired, Ms. Gabby. Go on inside and get some rest," he told her, yanking the cord and cranking it up.

Gabby bit her lip unsure of what to do, but she needed to get inside, feeling her cell vibrate yet again. She knew who it was, scurrying off to make it inside.

It didn't matter if she responded or not at this point. If Tyson was in a bad mood, he would somehow punish her. Some days a black eye, other days a busted lip. Not too much damage makeup couldn't cover, but if he got really rowdy, he might crack a rib or two.

She was used to it anyway because then the flowers, cards, candy and purses would come. He was loaded, too loaded for his own good, and he used that to replace the kind of love she really deserved.

It's the reason they landed at the New Year's party. Tyson ran a foundation for troubled youth that received thousands of dollars from investors. He'd somehow used his story and charm and before she knew it, Tyson's Kids was almost a nationwide household brand.

Many referrals came through Judge West's office. With that came more invitations to anything from charity golf tournaments down to private parties solely for a certain elite group of people. Tyson dibbled and dabbled in it a few times, but he mostly went to see whose pockets he could get in to donate to his foundation.

"Thanks, again! Good night!" she said, waving at him before she stuck her key in the door to go inside.

WHAP!

"Didn't I tell you about being so friendly to his ass? You have to be the most retarded bitch I know. Do I need to fucking remind you who the hell I am and whose bitch you are?" he asked, not really expecting an answer after delivering another blow to her mouth.

WHAP!

"Ugh!" she groaned, holding her mouth as she dropped her purse on the floor. "Uh, uh. I'm sorry."

"You damn right, you're sorry. A sorry, fat ass bitch that can't fuckin' respect her man," he hissed, breathing heavily.

He was still mad he had missed time at the office behind her. Ever since that night, he had to hire a public relations representative to put a spin on the story in the community. He knew whoever those men were, were well connected. No matter who he asked, even Judge West, he got no answers as to their identity.

All he knew was his woman seemed to be enjoying herself instead of sitting patiently and quietly for him like he told her to. This was his first year being invited and he wanted to make a great impression. Too bad that impression came with a hospital stay and a trip to the dentist.

"Okay," she whimpered, catching the blood on the back of her hand before it fell on the floor.

If it did, that would be one more thing he'd punish her for. One thing about Tyson was he was a neat freak. Things had to be in order at all times. One item moved or misplaced meant a belt whooping or a body slam, depending on his mood.

He was still recovering, but as he regained his strength, the beatings started up again. She stood quietly, waiting for him to dismiss her to make dinner. He wouldn't eat unless she made it fresh and served it on a hot plate.

"Good," he whispered, watching her stand there as she waited for his next set of instructions.

He then stroked her face, his thumb rubbing her slightly bruised cheek. She bit the inside of her lip, holding in any sign of pain. One sound or word indicating she was in pain was not tolerated. He dragged his hand down her face to her neck and squeezed it until she opened her mouth.

"So fucking beautiful," he hissed, lifting her face up by the chin and kissing her. He hummed, tasting her blood on her busted lip. "And sweet, too." He pecked her two times, telling her how much he loved her.

As required, she replied, "I love you more."

He answered, "Prove it."

Gabby began to unbutton her dress slowly in front of him, her size D breasts springing out, covered in a lace black bra. She dropped the dress just above her thick hips that he loved so much. Taking her time, she unhooked her bra and tossed it to the side.

"Yesss," he replied, watching her pierced, milk chocolate nipples greet him. "Come here."

He pulled her and sat back on the love seat, pulling her down. He cupped both of her breasts, squeezing them together as took both nipples in his mouth. She gasped, throwing her head back as he fed himself. The piercings were his idea, creating a tingling sensation as they grew bigger and harder for him.

"Ahhhh," she groaned, grinding on his center.

"You feel that big muhfucka?" he asked her, slipping one hand underneath the dress that hung around her waist. He slid her lace black panties to the side, and in one motion, he ripped them off.

"Uh!" she cried out, before he popped the rest of the buttons that held the rest of her dress around her waist. Now she was naked as the day she was born, her scent sending him into a frenzy. "Baby," she uttered, feeling him swell up even more. She slipped her hand down and pulled his dick out.

Stroking it, she rode him, sliding her pussy up and down the outside of the shaft. Anxious to feel the inside, he popped her hand.

Pop!

"That's enough. Fuck," he growled, tapping her thigh. "Ride this dick and you better not muhfuckin' stop until I say so. Hurry up!"

Just like that, the fantasy was gone. Sex was the only activity that sometimes showed the softer side of him. Well, unless he was drunk. Then it was rough and hard, but still it was better than being beaten.

Gabby quickly rose up just enough to land on the head, watching his eyes flicker with a crazed excitement. He couldn't take it anymore, bringing her down fast and hard. She screamed, panting as she tried to adjust to his massive girth. If she bragged on anything, it was the size of his dick. Truthfully, because she didn't have anything to compare it to, so to her it was pretty big.

Slapping her ass, Tyson grunted as he fucked her from underneath, biting and sucking her engorged nipples. He twirled one nipple ring on his tongue while slipping two fingers in her ass. Gabby lost it, going wild. He fucked her in both holes while forcing her to concentrate as he went through his interrogation.

"Un huh, can't nobody fuck you like I can," he spat, going harder and harder. "Now, what's rule number one, you nasty ass slut?" Tyson got a high off of calling her vulgar names. The look of fear in her eyes, easily sent him over the edge.

Pop, pop, pop!

"Uh, uh. No smiling and look—look forward at all times!" she screamed, feeling the sting from him slapping her travel up and down her body.

"That's right. Good answer," he told her, catching and biting her nipple as it bounced on his face with each pump.

"Uh!" she cried out, closing her eyes as he twirled it between his teeth and tongue.

"Shut the fuck up. Now, what's rule number two?" He stood up, squatting in the air as she rolled and grinded on his dick. "You know that turns me on. Shit, I love your ass. You're my little nasty bitch. Come on now. Talk to me."

"No—man can, can ta—talk to me... Mmmm," she moaned, closing her yes. "No man can talk to me unless, unless he speaks to you first," she managed to get out as he pinched her clitoris.

"Why?' he asked her, his balls slamming against her ass the faster he went.

"Be—because I'm your bitch!" she screamed.

"Arggh," he grunted forcefully, feeling her walls clench his dick. "That's right! You're my bitch!"

Gabby couldn't take it anymore, feeling her release threatening to unleash. She wanted to let go, but she couldn't until he said so. Tyson knew, too, laughing as her eyes fluttered, then rolled in the back of her head.

"Uh, baby. Mmmm," she whispered, shaking her head. "Can —can I?"

"Naw," he replied. "Not until I hear rule number three. And you better make sure that nigga outside hear it too, bitch, or I'ma beat your ass."

"Rule number three," she said, her voice shaking. "I belong to—to you and only y—you. The only way o—out is through—" she groaned, unsure if she could hold it in.

"Don't fuck with me," he warned her, slapping her hard three times on the ass.

Pow, pow, pow!

She screamed and shouted, "The only way out is through death!"

"That's it. I taught you well," he said, a devilish laugh escaping his lips. He dropped to his knees, laying her on the floor. "Now you can," he hissed, watching her jerked before he pulled out of her and crawled over her face.

"Suck this dick, fat bitch," he demanded, ramming it in her mouth. "Argghh!" He pumped and pumped until he exploded, filling her mouth with all of his seed. "Damn," he said, sighing as he gripped both of her jaws. "That's it, baby. Swallow my shit. Swallow all of it." He pinched her nose, feeling her throat open up. He rocked a few times, completely emptying himself.

He watched her eyes tear up, but she didn't dare move. That was rule number four. It applied to everything. Once you were in trouble, you never moved until he said so. He pulled himself out of her mouth and backed up just enough to grab her by the back of her neck.

He dropped his forehead to hers, feeling her heart rapidly beat. "Your heart's beating for me, baby?"

"Yes," she whispered, coughing as his thick cum was still lodged in the back of her throat. She swallowed once more and he smiled.

"You know I love you, right?" He closed his eyes before giving her a quick kiss.

"Yes."

"You know there's nothing I won't do for you, right?"

"Yes," she said again, tears filling up her eyes.

"Good. Listen up. I won't have to discipline you if you stop fucking with me, okay? Do what the hell I tell you to do and I promise, Gabby, I'll give you the world. This right here where we live is just the beginning. These clothes, that truck and all, just a tip of what I will give you.

I swear I would snatch down the fucking sky for you. Just keep them niggas out your face and your conversation over here. There's no need in telling you about my pussy. You know already," he said, laughing. "Right?"

"Yes, baby."

"Yeah, I know. I'll fuck you while you're six feet under if you even think about it. Even there, you're still mine. Now," he said, standing up over her as he helped her up. "The next time, I may not let you off so easy. Go clean yourself up then fix me something to eat."

He popped her in the side of her hip, before dismissing her. Before she left the living room, he stopped her.

"Oh, be sure you don't cry when you find out Mr. Morgan is dead. Just make his wife one of them red velvet cakes you make so good. I'll even get a nice arrangement. I figured that's the least I can do since he's being friendly and helpful."

Tyson laughed, aiming his hand like a gun towards the window at Mr. Morgan. Catching a glimpse of him through the window, he tipped his hat at him and waved as he continued to cut their lawn.

CHAPTER NINE

X couldn't believe he'd let Ace talk him into going to the strip club after the week he had. He lost his big case, having to file for another trial in a different venue. He knew with Jessica he could have won, but she was now working for the attorney that represented the plaintiff.

They spent weeks working late hours but somehow, after she left, he missed an important piece of evidence related to DNA. Not one to blame, X decided ultimately it was his fault, but something about Jessica was off even before she was let go.

Then he and Reagan weren't on the best of terms. She had a minor setback, but agreed to work for him to handle his finances, more than qualified with her master's in finance. She had a sponsor, but most nights she told them she was too busy to go to a meeting.

Instead of talking to his parents, he kept their interactions simple. The only time he stopped by was to pick up and drop Reagan off to work. By this time, she had earned her driver's license back after a long suspension, but she still preferred being chauffeured around.

"You a'ight? Standing there like you don't know what to do," Ace said to him, slapping the stripper named Milky Way on the ass. X knew they had an arrangement since she was the only reason they even came that deep south.

She bent over, her freshly shaved pussy opening up like a flower for all to see, with her tongue out. Ace lost it, gripping both of her ass cheeks, opening her up even wider.

"You wild, yo," X said, laughing at him. Back in college, he would have found her something he could stick his dick in and play with, but he wasn't feeling it honestly.

He wasn't judging and believe it or not, X liked his women a little rough around the edges, even street smart, but could hold an intelligent conversation. That was Jessica in some ways, but she was young and childish. Hadn't lived enough life, and honestly, she was a little too hood.

He could see them being a Ike and Tina before before they realized how they really didn't need to do anything but worked together. She was hardheaded, too. Something he needed less of.

Ace popped her on the ass two more times and Milky Way started bouncing her ass up and down in his face. Ace leaned down, stopping just barely in front of it, blowing inside her pussy.

When she shot and looked over her shoulder, she slowly wound her hips to Beenie Man's "Who Am I?", a reggae club favorite. Everyone jumped up to the popular reggae throwback, strippers now working the room even harder.

Tooley made his way to the stage when this stripper who went by the name of Rainbow came out. She was on the tiny side, but swirled her hips in slow motion like that made his dick rise. On her nipples were beaded jewels the color of a rainbow and true to her name, she had a rainbow tattooed around her waist.

Tooley was known for finding talent, so many of the local deejays, rappers or up and coming producers knew him. The deejay shouted him out and Rainbow like a snake, made her way over to him. Out came his roll of money as he pulled a seat up to the edge of the stage.

"X, you better get in on that," Ace said, rubbing his hard-on against Milky Way's ass. By now, she was milky, so X already knew what was next.

"Nigga, you better watch yourself," X stood up and whispered in his ear. "This not us no more. Either wife this bitch and make her your girl or move around. She may be for everybody, bruh."

"Shut up," Ace told him, biting his bottom lip as she reached behind herself rubbing his manhood. "We're in a damn strip club, not work. In here, we're niggas. Drop your fucking law degree and feel on some pussy, my man."

Ace was the best at what he did just like X. Unlike him, however, he easily moved in and out of both worlds. He upheld the law, but when needed to, he did what he had to do to catch the bad guys. Finding tips and building relationships in strips clubs proved to be very helpful, especially meeting Milky Way.

After they met, he knew getting close and comfortable with civilians gave him an advantage when he needed to squeeze information out from the streets. That was very critical to his success. Even being close to a few bouncers who were great intel, watching the dope boys come in and pop bottles, spending a shit load of money.

"Suit your fucking self," X said, being the grouch that he was. They all wished he was still with Avery now. At least they wouldn't have to deal with his bullshit ass mood in a room full of pussy.

"Don't act like that. We all gotta do things sometimes to stay above it all," he reminded him, raising his eyebrows. "Yeaaah," X hissed, dismissing him that quickly as Milky Way purred, subtly playing with herself. No one but Ace could see it, but it turned him on.

X grilled him, clenching his teeth. It was true what Ace said, but he wasn't feeling the scene. This wasn't him after being with Avery for three years. He was starting to realize that maybe he was a one woman man. To make the time past, he decided to shake it off, figuring a little dance wouldn't hurt.

"Fuck it," he said. "You're right, I might be trippin'."

"No, you are, just like Gator. All over there drinking his feelings away. I don't know what your sister got, but I'm glad I don't want it."

"Watch it," X told him, picking up his drink.

Ace licked his lips then smiled as Milky Way turned around and dropped down in front of him. She slid her hand between his legs, cupping his balls.

"You want some of this dick in your life, don't you?" Milky Way nodded, letting him know it was time to go to the private room. "X, watch Tooley and Gator. I'll be back." He pulled Milky Way up by her hair, whispering in her ear. She giggled and turned around, tugging him by his shirt.

X waved him off, before a random stripper he'd never seen before stopped and asked him if he wanted a dance. She seemed nervous like it was her first night, so he spared her. His attitude was bad, but he knew she was just trying to make her money. "Yeah, let me see what's up with you."

Surprised, she said, "Uh, okay."

She looked around, watching the other girls, but had no problem mimicking their moves. Her mocha-colored skin, smooth and shiny, made the yellow thong and top pop. Her eyes, the weirdest green color, lured him in. He relaxed in his chair, sliding down just enough for her to stand in between them.

She leaned over and in a baby-like voice said, "They call me Glitter."

"Less talking, love. We're not friends," he told her. "I'm paying for a dance, not conversation."

While X decided to just go with it and "fake pretend" like he was into her, Tooley was about to bend Rainbow over.

"You like that, daddy?" Rainbow asked him, climbing back on stage on all fours.

"Hell yeah," he said huskily, pulling her back just enough to where her pussy sat right in his face. Tooley was drunk. He drank the most out of all of them, tonight tossing back a bottle of Don Julio by himself.

"That's my bitch, motherfucka. No hands," he heard in his ear, turning to the side. He chuckled watching this feisty, pretty female in a wheelchair. She was a stud, but if she was down, Tooley was ready to play with the both of them.

"Calm down, shorty." He curled his lip, a sly smile appearing. "It's just a dance. If she's yours, she still will be when it's over unless you—"

Bam!

Before he could finish, Kaleela head butted him and pulled out her nine. Rainbow screamed, quickly sliding down in front of her. "Baby, you're drunk. Stop it, please. You're fucking up my money."

"Bitch, you don't need this money," she snarled. "You like shaking your ass, then making me feel bad about fucking other hoes. Fuck you and him," she told her, lowering her tool and backing up. "Yo, you can have her ass. My name's Kaleela if you want these problems. I'll settle the bill for that knot resting on yo' shit."

Kaleela took off, the room still jumping. Rainbow fell down next to him, apologizing as he tried to sit up. Tooley was mad he'd let a female catch him off guard like that, shaking his head as he tried to focus.

She helped him to the section where X and Gator were as he pointed to it. He plopped down, resting his head back when X realized something was off.

"What the hell happened to him?" he yelled, pushing Glitter out of the way.

"My—my," Rainbow said, now crying. "I—I'm sorry," she whispered and took off, getting lost in the crowd.

"Gator!" X screamed his way. "Watch his ass!" he told Gator, snapping him out of his thoughts. "Let me go get Ace! I knew we shouldn't have come to this shit."

Gator gritted his teeth looking at him as he stood up. He was texting Reagan, threatening her to be home when he got there. She'd been ignoring him, but tonight he was about to fuck some shit up if she didn't let him in.

Ace came out sweating, looking around until he saw Tooley laid back with his eyes closed. "Shit! Who did it, bruh? Show me where he's at?" Ace carried whether he was on duty or not, pulling his unofficial, unassigned revolver out.

Gator somewhat saw the whole thing, but his mind was on Reagan. Still, he got a chuckle out of it.

"Aye," he whispered, walking up to the both of them, "I think it was a female."

"A female?" Ace shot back, while X frowned.

"Yeah, I caught a glimpse of the two of them at the stage." Tooley's face proved he was right, too.

X was pissed for real now. "This some bullshit. I'm out. Y'all grab him and let's go."

While Ace continued to probe, yelling at Tooley, X walked out. They had two minutes to follow him or he was leaving all of them.

CHAPTER TEN

"Where is she?" Shona said, whipping into the parking lot. She was still on the phone with Ace, hearing his boys talking and fussing in the background.

"That's you in the Rolls Royce Phantom, now?" he asked, eyeing it as soon as the lights glared brightly in his face.

"Yup," she said, stopping and parking as she hopped out. Ace knew for sure they were sitting on some serious money, not legal money either. His boys did, too, raising their eyebrows.

"Damn," X said lowly, watching her walk towards them in a t-shirt, tights and slides. She was still beautiful, her hair all over her head as she snatched her silk bonnet off.

"Damn is right," Tooley said, rubbing the knot on his forehead.

Hood at its best, yet she was still beautiful, her hair all over her head once she realized she still had her satin bonnet on. She snatched it off quickly, her hair falling effortlessly, causing them all to be in awe.

"Sisssss! Sis, help!" Kaleela yelled at her, laughing while Ace had her wheelchair locked. "These bitches don't know who they are fucking with! I'm a motherfucking boss! An original crew member!" she giggled, pulling up her pants leg to show her nine.

"Shut the fuck up," she said to her, approaching Ace. "Thanks for the call. Tow that shit or leave it at this point. I really don't care one way or another. Uncuff the chair and we'll be out of your way."

"Like that?" X dared to ask. The way he saw it, his boy did her ratchet ass sister favor. She not only could be arrested for aggravated assault and battery, but carrying a weapon he was sure wasn't registered or clean.

Turning her head slowly his way, a sly grin appeared on her face. She wasn't in the mood for the needy sidekick wanting to be seen. But since he wanted attention, she decided to oblige him.

"Most definitely like that," she said sultrily, walking up towards him. "And you can help him," Shona almost whispered, her eyes riding up and down his body. He was fine, but she still wasn't impressed with his rude ass. Looks were just that—looks.

"See, there you go," she all but cooed as he stood damn near paralyzed. Shona was the shit. Even he could tell no matter that satin bonnet screamed. "Now I have spoken to you, so I guess it does pay to be the help."

"The help? Bi—"

"Aye," Ace stopped him, grabbing him forearm. "Chill." He knew her kind working the streets. She'd easily fuck them up if they let her. Even though he could have arrested her sister, he was tired of seeing his black women locked up. Especially one in a wheelchair. He could tell she was drunk, hoping she'd sleep it off.

"Fuck that," X growled lowly, snatching his arm back as she approached Kaleela, kneeling down in her face.

X squinted his eyes, his mouth now in an "O" shape as he watched all that ass spread wide when she did. Just that fast, a nice butterfly tattoo above all that ass against her high-yellow skin complexion made him wince.

"I gave you time, but no more. Tomorrow, rehab or you're out, Kaleela. I can't keep doing this shit," she fussed, extending her hand towards Ace. "Hand me the key," she told Ace when she saw he hadn't moved.

"Uh, excuse me but I can't give you these keys. She's drunk."

"She's always drunk," she said, looking at him with an attitude. "I got this. It's why you called me, right?"

"And she's dick deprived! She always mad! Ahh haa!" Kaleela shouted, laughing before she started puking.

Blahhhh! Ugh! Blahhhh!

"Damn," X said, frowning as he covered his mouth. Sadly, he understood her plight, remembering how wasted Reagan could get. Even Gator shot her a dirty look, walking off to call Reagan once again.

"Shit," Shona said lowly, jumping back then rubbing her sister's back. "K baby, you got to stop baby."

Just that quickly, she went from being angry to concerned and nurturing. She loved her sister to no end, but she was slowly killing herself.

X caught her tearing up, wanting to help but he didn't. He knew how this ended but from the looks of it, Shona was an enabler when it came to dealing with family members with an addiction.

"Here," X told her, handing her some wet wipes he took from the glove box of his car. Just like that, his anger was gone. His head was fucked up watching another sibling live the life he has lived most of his adult years. "These come in handy, you know?"

"Thank you," she whispered, taking them as she pulled Kaleela's head back. She was damn near in tears herself. "I'm so—"

"We're good," X told her, holding up both hands.

After wiping her mouth, Ace bent down and uncuffed the wheelchair.

"So about the truck, I can get it towed for free. Just shoot me the address," Ace told Shona. "I see this shit ain't as simple as I thought. My bad, shorty."

"Tell me about it," she said while Kaleela laughed loudly, shouting obscenities at them.

Shona stood up, wishing she could leave it but she couldn't do her sister like that. It was always Shona and Kaleela and it always would be.

"Okay, that would be nice." Besides, the last time she had it towed, it cost her three hundred dollars. She had it but this was proving to be something she couldn't waste money on anymore.

"And take my card. You know I got your number. Let's stay in touch," Ace offered up. Strangely, X was feeling some type of way, checking Shona out for himself.

He chuckled to himself, shaking his head. This is Ace. He was a savior. A savior for people caught up in the streets or in bad situations, so he couldn't trip. He even put himself on the line for him one time, a line that could have landed him in a prison for life, pushing that dark memory to the back of his mind.

"Okay." She gave them a weak smile before rolling Kaleela to her car. After getting her in, she put her wheelchair in the deep trunk. Luckily for her, it was big enough to hold it. Once she and her wheelchair were secured, she was about to get in until X decided to stop her.

"Aye, I fuck hard with my sister. She's got her a little issue, too. Don't be an enabler or you'll be a part of the problem," he caught himself saying before he realized what he had said. "I'm just saying."

She sucked her teeth and curled the left side of her lip up. "An enabler? I look like an enabler because I chose to show up for her. Fuck out of here," she snarled, slamming her door.

X nodded his head, deciding to let it go. He knew she was, deciding she needed time to realize it like he did. He just hoped she did before they both figured out it was too late.

X scratched his head, wishing that turned out better. He wanted to ask for her number, but something told him he would see her again in the future. He could ask Ace, but that was some straight stalker shit to him.

"I see you," Ace said and smiled, watching X as his eyes followed Shona's car until he couldn't see them anymore.

"Naw, I just know how fucked up it is when your people just keep fucking up. But I can't lie," he said lowly, grinning. "She finer than a motherfucker."

"Hell, yeah," Ace said, smiling. He was glad X seemed to be interested in somebody. While he enjoyed fucking on hoes, he knew his boy. X was ready for something stable, something serious, hoping he could link the two of them up at some point.

Boom!

Shona jumped up out of her sleep, snatching Pink Lady from

underneath her pillow. It had been a month since she had to get her from the strip club, drunk out of her mind. She heard a loud crash right outside. The last thing she remembered was falling asleep with a glass of Chardonnay in her hand.

It had been a long day at the shop. She was desperately looking for one more beautician, one that could braid. That would free up some of her time, allowing her to book more clients. She wasn't friendly and she knew her past came with enemies.

She could do manicure and pedicures, but she hated touching feet. She hesitated putting up a help wanted sign, but did just before she left. Kaleela, like most Friday or Saturday nights, was out. Most times it was with one of her hoes or at a strip club.

For the clubs she frequented the most, Shona paid the owner monthly to call her up in case Kaleela got drunk and out of control. Her new favorite spot, Tastee's, was her go to one on the north end but as of late Teddy Riley, the owner, told her he hadn't seen her.

Shona didn't know why he called himself that since he was 6'5", weighing over three hundred pounds, but he did. She knew Kaleela would soon mess up, but like always, she waited for when she needed to bail her out.

After the last strip club incident, she eased up on drinking, so Shona stopped stressing her about rehab. Sadly, without saying it, she knew she was exactly what X called her, an enabler. She just didn't know how to be anything different. All she knew was the streets and Kaleela; the streets she left behind the morning Chico walked out of her living room.

Hearing the loud sound outside, she soon learned that she was wrong. Taking off on her feet, she rushed to the front door, her .22 coming out first.

She almost fell, stopping short of Kaleela's Tahoe that sat about three feet from the front door. She saw a trail of trees down and their flowerbed that was now destroyed. There sat Kaleela, laughing.

"Kaleela! Really?" she shouted, walking around to the driver's door. "What the hell is going on? You're trying to kill yourself or better yet, bring heat our way out here? You know black people either squatting or trapping in their eyes to live out here," she gritted, snatching her arm.

She snatched back, sucking her teeth. "Damn, girl. Why are you yelling and shit?"

Shona could smell the liquor through her pores, her eyes bloodshot red. She knew talking to her was useless, but it didn't mean she wasn't about to handle her right then.

"Get your ass out," she yelled, pressing the button that lifted her wheelchair from underneath the truck before it lowered back down. It cost about twenty grand to get that installed, but it was worth it, giving Kaleela some independence. Now, she had lost it as far as Shona was concerned. This was it.

"Bruh, why you yelling though?" she said, giggling until she saw how upset her sister was. "Never mind, you're right. I fucked up. Just remind me tomorrow I'm not fucking with Rainbow's hoe ass no mo'.

That bitch made me think she quit dancing, but naw. She still down south, shaking her ass and showing my pussy. You wonder why I say fuck them hoes? Well, she's why. I guess that's what I get for wifing a stripper. Fuck that bitch!" A tear threatened to fall before she caught it.

Shona sighed, walking up to her. She was still mad, but it hurt her even more seeing how messed up Kaleela was behind love.

"Well, her loss, K baby."

She gave her a hug. Kaleela resisted at first, but soon gave in, crying on her shoulder. She rubbed her back, letting her rest her face on her chest. She must have cried for about ten minutes before she stopped and sat up, wiping her face.

Immediately, she put on her killer face. "I'm good. Let me get out," she said.

Shona stepped back, watching her wheelchair drop. She struggled getting in, still inebriated. With Shona's help, she sat down but had trouble pushing through the grass.

"Yo, you gone help me or what?" she snapped with a scowl on her face.

Shona laughed, watching how quickly Kaleela's mood changed. "I'm helping now, but tomorrow we've got to have a serious talk,

Kaleela. I'm serious *this time*." She gave Kaleela that look, waiting for her to respond.

"A'ight, tomorrow though," she said and nodded. "I'm about to call this hoe and cuss her out before I do," she told her, punching Rainbow's number once she got in the house. "I'ma murder that hoe."

On the first ring, she picked up crying. "Oh boy," Shona whispered, quickly pushing Kaleela to the bathroom to get her washed up and in bed. She felt sorry for Kaleela, but right about now she feared what would happen to Rainbow if she showed up.

CHAPTER ELEVEN

"Fired?" Tyson repeated, glaring at Gabby. She went to work at Macy's department store after six years and was let go today. That particular store was soon going out of business, the employees at the top making the higher salaries being laid off first.

"No, no," she said, correcting herself as she watched him get upset. "Laid off. I—I told you about it a like four months ago over the holidays. Remember the meeting where they mentioned the company was experiencing a decrease in sales?"

"I did, but what did I tell you?" he barked, slamming his hand down on the table.

Tonight she made his favorite, lamb with a side of garlic mashed potatoes and steamed broccoli. She also made a pan of banana nut muffins with freshly brewed, sweet iced tea. She had hoped making his favorite meal would soften the blow, but clearly it hadn't.

"I tried," she said, squirming in her chair.

Lately, Tyson had been complaining about a loss in donations for his foundation. After his fight the night of New Year's Eve, he noticed a few of his investors had pulled out. It shocked him even more when Judge West's assistant contacted him, advising that they had a change in their vision. That also meant their money would now go too.

"So you're telling me old ass Mack who's constantly sweating you every time I see him, couldn't save your job? The first time you mentioned it to me, I told you to go and put that pussy on him, didn't I?" He slammed his fist down on the table once more and stood up.

Gabby's heart started racing. She knew he may not have taken the news well, but not only had she made his favorite meal, but she was even ready to become Eva, her alter ego, scantily dressed in her purple, satin negligee.

She'd gone as far as to curl her hair, the thick wavy curls draping over her shoulder touching her plump breasts. Her perfumed, shimmery lotion on her skin was a nice added touched. She'd recently pierced her clitoris, a request of his. It was the only thing he actually made her do she was pleased with. It heightened and quickened both of their orgasms, ending the time he spent inside of her.

Tyson smiled when he first saw her after a long day at work, smelling the aroma of food in the kitchen. He smacked her ass, eager to get through the meal. Now he was pissed.

He walked towards her, pulling his thick belt through the loops. He slowly wrapped it around his hand. "Stand up."

Gabby hesitated, unsure if she should make a run for it or take it and get it over with. "Baby..." she said, her voice trailing off, and she took in a deep breath.

"Get up now!" he demanded.

As soon as she did, he grabbed her by the arm and swung her around, hitting her over and over all over her back.

"Didn't I tell you what would happen if you lost that damn job, bitch?" he screamed, now hitting her on her thighs and legs as she fell on the floor.

Gabby screamed as she tried to shelter her body, covering her face while her arms, back and legs took lashes that broke her skin. "Ahhhhh! Ah, ah, ah, ah," she cried out, wishing she were anywhere but here. Even death was a comparable option to her if it meant she would be free of him.

Then she felt something hot, wet, and warm as he laughed wickedly. She looked up and there he stood, his penis over her body as he released his urine all over her body. After shaking it to release the last of it, he issued a swift and hard kick in her stomach.

Bam!

Gabby felt her ribs crack. Her mouth was wide open, but no sound came out as she tried to absorb the pain all at once. Her eyes wide open, saw him smile. He appeared pleased with his handiwork.

"Tomorrow, call him," he told her, zipping his dress pants up. "If you can't get it back, find something. Don't just sit around here being a useless bitch, Gabby. Now clean yourself up. Then I might let you suck my dick."

He stepped over her, walking out of the kitchen as she laid there and cried.

The next day, Gabby finally chose to leave. Many days she would pack a bag and all of her important documents only to go to work and return home. But this time was different. As soon as he was out the door, rushing off to go and see someone, she was right behind him.

She had no job to go to and even if she did, the pain was unbearable. After packing a small duffle bag with a few clothing items, toiletries and her financial documents, she managed to drive herself to the bank.

Dressed suspiciously in a sweat suit in ninety degree weather, Gabby held it together long enough to close out her accounts before driving to another bank and opening up another one.

She whipped into the emergency room garage and cried out to anyone that would help her. The stares alerted her that the police would soon be there as they got louder and louder, still no one helped. She left her cell and all of her belongings back at the house after Tyson got up and went to the office.

She whimpered, walking in slowly into the emergency room where an older woman old enough to be her grandmother smiled and greeted her. "Welcome to Mercy Hospital. How can I help you?"

"I—I need help," she murmured, breaking down once more.

The woman jumped up and swiftly walked around the counter,

touching her arm. Gabby screamed and pulled away, holding it. "Ouch! Ah, ah, ah, ah."

"Oh no," the woman said, realizing this was more than the usual. Looking around, she decided to take her to a private examination area. "Betty, watch the front. I need to head to Room B." Room B was reserved for law enforcement, whenever a crime resulting in injuries was suspected.

"Of course."

"Come on, sweetheart," she said, motioning for Gabby to follow her. She gently closed the door, pointing to the examination bed. "Let's start with your name."

Gabby hesitated, second-guessing now if she should even be here. Her plan was to ride all the way north on I-95, heading out of Florida. She could barely breathe, her bruised ribs causing her to have a shortness of breath.

"Well, my name is Nurse Earvin. Lillie Mae, to be exact. I've got two daughters, both just as pretty as you are. And let me tell you, if they were here instead of you, I pray to God someone would do everything humanly possible to make sure they were safe.

They are both grown and on their own, but sometimes things happen and it's easy to lose your way. Does that sound familiar?" she asked her, hoping that would encourage her to open up.

Gabby, holding her center, nodded her head yes. Nurse Earvin walked over to her and softly rubbed her back. "Thank you," she whispered, taking slow and deep breaths.

"No need to thank me. Here, let me step out and get the doctor. While I'm gone, take everything off and lay down. There's a gown. Since we are meeting for the first time and honesty is important, I must tell you that if it seems like someone is a victim of a crime, we call law enforcement."

She watched Gabby's eyes buck as her head shot up. "No, no. It's routine. No one is in trouble. It's just to take a statement as to what happened, but no matter what, before you leave, we will make sure you are okay. Sounds fair?"

"Yeah, I guess so," she said, taking the hospital gown and tie wrap.

"Very well. I'll be back."

An hour later, the doctor had completed a thorough examination. It was a classic case of domestic dispute gone physical, but Gabby wouldn't give much details. Thankfully, her ribs were only bruised. She was given a sedative and her injuries were cleaned and bandaged up.

She woke up a few hours later with a massive headache when she saw a man standing over her.

"Ah!" she screamed, jumping up before she snatched the cover over head body. When she did, she groaned, feeling the pain run throughout her body. "What, huh, who—
"

"Shhhh," he said in a soothing tone. "Calm down, Gabriela. I'm sorry if I scared you. I'm Detective Ace Alexander with the City of Miami Police Department." He knew exactly who she was, fighting hard to keep it together. The signs of a battered woman were there that night, he knew it and was ashamed of himself for even letting her walk.

At first, she didn't recognize him, but after studying his face, she realized she did. She lowered her blanket just a little, but she felt embarrassed, avoiding eye contact. She was hoping he didn't remember her, but it was clear that he did seeing the expression on his face. She could tell he wasn't pleased, fighting hard to maintain what he felt as he studied her injuries. All the while, she felt shame.

The night they'd met, he was charming, somewhat flirty but very easygoing. Although they'd only spoke briefly, she remembered how much she enjoyed the friendly interaction. She so wished she were back there that night when he first approached her, but fairytales didn't happen to woman like Gabby. No, beatings did and him being there was proof enough.

Ace could tell she was uncomfortable. That alone, angered him even more. He knew her thoughts, the thoughts of a woman that was broken from beating after beating. No grown woman needed to feel that way, especially when she hadn't done anything wrong.

"May I go off the record?" he asked, finding a gentler approach as he did his best to offer up a smile. He pulled up a chair and sat down, then scooted closer to her.

Gabby, confused by what he was asking, looked his way, then back down as she tugged on her blanket even more.

"Gabriela," he said lowly, leaning closer. He watched her nervously play with the edge of her blanket. He lifted both hands, carefully placing them down on top of the blanket until she stopped. "May I go off the record, meaning this is not an official conversation?"

"It's Gabby," she finally said. "I go by Gabby and sure...I guess."

Ace got up and made sure the door was locked before sitting back down. She was just as beautiful today as she was the night he met her a few months back. He struggled for over an hour about what to do, waiting for her to wake up. As soon as he saw her, he told the other detective to take the other call they'd gotten. Someone came in right before her, a gunshot victim. He was just glad it wasn't her and more importantly, she wasn't dead.

"Listen up. All I need is your permission to handle him. Once you tell me yes, it's done." Ace could tell she had questions, struggling with what he said. So he continued to talk, making sure she understood. "You remember who I am?"

She felt herself smiling, but caught herself. "Yes, I do."

When she smiled, he felt a tightness in his chest. *Who could hurt someone as sweet as her*, he thought to himself, wanting to touch her. Even in pain and bruised up, she had an aura about her that made him want to protect her. He also knew she was the kind of woman to be loyal, even to the man that had harmed her.

He decided to go out on a limb and take a different approach. He had enough ways to handle Tyson, but what he couldn't risk was her going back.

"I'm glad."

"Detective Alexander?" the doctor said, knocking on the door.

Immediately, Gabby looked afraid hearing the loud knocks on the door. Ace knew he had to do what was next then. "Relax, it's Dr. Roman." Opening the door, he allowed him in. "Yes, Dr. Roman?"

"I just wanted to check in with the patient before I go," he said, seeing the tense look on his face.

Dr. Roman, just like Nurse Earvin, had seen way too many domestic violence cases come in through their emergency room. Often they didn't share much, but he had hoped Ace was able to get something.

"Sure, but I can't step out. I'm still asking questions. Will that be a problem?" he asked, hoping it wasn't because he refused to leave her now.

"Miss Wilcox, may I speak freely in front of Detective Alexander?" he asked, her checking her vitals.

"I guess," she said again. Ace figured she wasn't sure of much, but he hoped to changed that. She then sat up just a little, looking at him as he gave her a warm smile. "Yes, you can."

"Very well. When patients come in with the injuries like yours, it's standard we do a rape treatment kit. I see you signed for it even though you advised us you weren't raped.

I'm sorry to say the results indicate you have gonorrhea. We are required to give this information to the Center for Disease Control. It's a way to track statistics, but also to ensure all partners are informed. Can we—"

"I'm afraid you can't, Doc," Ace answered for her, watching Gabby tear up as he stopped him. "This is a possible criminal case. You cannot share anything that could hinder this investigation. So, if that is all, I would like to finish speaking with Miss Wilcox alone."

He cleared his throat, nodding his head, and smiled.

"That's fine." He patted her on the shoulder, silently apologizing. "Miss Wilcox, you will be here a few days, but we plan to treat it with antibiotics. Before you leave, we will retest you. And Detective Alexander, thank you for all you do. You both have a good night."

After he closed the door, Ace locked it. "I'm sorry for butting in, but as far as I'm concerned, you're dead to that nigga. If he got a dirty dick, so let the next bitch have him."

Gabby broke down. She couldn't understand why all of this was happening to her. Ace reached for some tissue nearby, handing them to her to wipe her face and blow her nose.

"Off the record, you are getting discharged to my spot." Gabby stopped mid-stroke, wiping her eyes about to protest. "Don't even start. That's not optional. Where is your cell?"

"I don't have it. I left it at his place," she told him, still processing everything that happened over the past two days.

"I'll be back later with one. It will have my number and my address only under my contact information. I feel somewhat responsible. You already know the night he tried me, I should have put him in the ground.

Any man that could even touch you unless he's making love to you or holding your hand, little shit like that is a bitch ass nigga. Don't call anyone you know because trust me, he's pressing them for information. Do not talk to anyone else, not even someone from my office."

Grabbing his notepad, he sat down and took a deep breath. "Okay, now I need an official statement. Tell me what happened or what you remember *if anything?*" he added, hoping she caught on.

"I don't remember," she quickly said.

"So," he replied, writing in his notepad. "You don't remember. Were you drinking, had a long day at work, or anything that could *impair your memory?*"

"Yes, I was drinking," she said, catching on as she followed his line of questioning. "A lot. I blacked out and when I woke up, I was in pain. I don't know who could've done it."

"Dating anyone or having conflict with somebody, a friend or neighbor. *Maybe a boyfriend?*"

"Nope," she replied, matter-of-factly. "No boyfriend, but there have been some reported break-ins in my neighborhood."

"Okay, so what I got is you were drinking, passed out and recently, there have been break-ins in your neighborhood. Does that sound about right?" he asked, rubbing her shoulder. He was proud she caught on so quickly.

"Yeah, that's sounds about right," she said, unsure what she was doing. She didn't have a lot of options, cutting her family off years ago because of Tyson. She had some money, but no clue about where to start. Tyson was her world, controlling everything. She wasn't ready to allow another man to do that, but she didn't feel she had a solid enough plan to say no.

"Great. Here's my card. Remember, I'm Detective Ace Alexander."

He stood up and smiled, slipping his notebook inside his pocket. As soon as he did, his smile dropped. "What size do you wear?"

"Wh—why?" She shifted underneath the blanket, feeling self-conscious about her body. Ace sighed, reminding himself she just didn't realize the beauty she possessed, and he hated that.

"Gabby, you need clothes. I peeped the bag you brought in here. No matter what size, it doesn't matter 'cause you sexy as fuck. Now, tell me what size. Shoe size, too.

I mean I can have you barefoot and pregnant this time next month, but you know, I need to at least know all I can about my baby mama before we take it there," he said, teasing her about the baby mama part.

Ace loved pussy, but he was allergic to kids. He loved other people's kids, but he was nowhere near ready to have his own.

"In shoes, I wear an eight. A sixteen—" she said, sighing, "—in bottoms and for tops, an extra-large. I'm kinda big." A nervous laugh followed, but he stopped her.

"And gorgeous, shit. And kind and he's a fucking fool. So do me a favor and kill any negative thoughts from here on out," he told her.

She could see the stressed lines in his forehead. Ace was smooth, always knowing what to say but today she could tell he meant what he said with a sense of urgency.

"Okay," she whispered.

"Remember, speak to no one about this case. We've got someone on the door. Sleep easy, Gabriela."

"You're coming back, right?" she quickly asked him, feeling anxious. She didn't realize how his presence added some level of comfort until he was about to leave.

"I will always come back for you," he told her, taking and squeezing her hand. "Now, get some rest. I got some shopping to do."

Gabby watched him leave, admiring how good he looked now that she saw him dressed casually in a pair of dark gray pair of jeans, a Black t-shirt and a pair of gray and black Js.

CHAPTER TWELVE

"Shona, where is your sister?" Chaney asked, popping her gum as she chewed. She knew Shona hated it, but she'd been quiet all morning and a quiet Shona wasn't a safe one.

Shona knew why she was asking. Chaney was one of Kaleela's bitches. She was also one of the best cosmetologists in Miami, but she was loud and ghetto. People came from all over seeking her services. When Shona first opened up The Palace about five years ago, she was determined to get nothing but the best.

To find the best talent, anyone she saw with a nice hairdo, she stopped and ask who did their hair. After hearing Chaney's name from almost every other person, she called her up and made her an offer she couldn't refuse.

Chaney was used to doing hair in her house, right on her grandmother's front porch. She could have paid a house off two times with the money she brought in, but Chaney couldn't see outside of the world she grew up in.

Throwing in nothing but the best hair and products with the option to make her own prices, Chaney quickly took up Shona's offer and they'd been making history ever since.

Celebrities from all over came there and even though Shona tried to stay off the social media radar, her name soon popped up. Still, she kept a low profile sending most of them Chaney's way.

"Chaney, one, you're chewing like a damn cow. Stop it. I've told you this," she said, rolling her eyes. She was doing her first sew-in for the day, only getting there thirty minutes ago. "It's distracting and it's rude. Ma'am, I'm so sorry," she said to her client.

"Girl, relax. It's not that serious. I was just asking. That's all," she replied, spitting it out.

She pulled out her makeup bag and touched up her makeup. Chaney was what many called high-yellow. She looked almost like Tiny from Escape, short of the nose. Hers was long and slender and she had large, Bambi-like eyes.

Her hair, never the same, drew attention without her even trying. It was her way of branding herself. Today, it was braided into skinny braids in a Mohawked style, blue with gold tips. She had on a skin tight, white fitted dress with gold and blue Converse and no underwear.

Shona knew she was waiting for Kaleela, but she wasn't coming. The night after she almost ran into the house was it for her. The next morning, Shona found a rehab, forcing her to check in.

While she was sleep, Shona took all of her guns, forcing her to go. If she didn't, the only option was putting her out and cutting her off. Kaleela decided to go, but cursed her out the entire way there.

"Maybe she's with Rainbow," Remy said under her breath. Remy was her other cosmetologist.

Unlike them, Remy was married to her high school sweetheart. She loved her some Reggie. They had two kids that were Remy's world. Dark skin with full lips and dimples, Remy was what many called cute. She also had the smallest waist but largest booty. She religiously wore her hair bone straight with a part down the middle.

"Or Reggie," Chaney shot back.

"Play with someone else. We don't have those problems in our life, bitch," she countered playfully even though she was serious. Chaney had hands, so they all knew not to push her buttons.

"You're sure?" she asked her, raising one eyebrow.

Watching it about to go left, Shona chimed in. "Look, Chaney. You got a ten o'clock coming, but you rolled up in here at eight. Either you can go color a few bundles while you wait or act like you didn't just come early to see Kaleela. She's fine. If she wants to holler at you, she will. And you, Remy," she said, looking her way with a scowl. " Stop being messy. You already know how Chaney is."

"Gosh, I was just playing. Why is she being so messy? Everyone knows Reggie not pressed for nothing. I got everything he need. Reggesha and Reggie Rozay are his life." Remy's client giggled at her kids' names until she snatched her thread through tightly.

"Ouch!" she said, flinching.

"Oh boo, I'm sorry. It got stuck." Remy stuck her tongue out at her behind her back, getting caught by Shona who mouthed for her to stop. She mouthed back "okay", but she was in a funk now. She made a mental note to ask Reggie if he knew anyone by the name of Rainbow.

"This girl," Chaney mumbled, walking to the back. "I got you, boss lady. Let me go and color this hair."

She smiled and tilted her head. "Why thank you. Shelby, you're good?" she asked the girl she hired about a week ago mostly to do braids. She wasn't much of a talker, but she knew how to do some hair.

"I'm good, boss lady," she said in her natural baby-like voice.

Shelby was twenty-five, but if you closed your eyes, you would think she was a kid. She had big button eyes that blinked every time she spoke. Barely five feet tall, it was hard not to pat her head because she was so cute.

An hour later, an unfamiliar woman walked in looking over her shades. She had an air about her that screamed celebrity, but Shona couldn't place her face as she thought about local celebrities.

She was tall, dark and damn near flawless with not one hair out of place. Shona's receptionist, Marilyn, was bobbing her head listening to music. The woman placed her large, Louis Vuitton bag on the counter, waiting to be acknowledged.

Shona knew her purse was no knock off. Hell, she'd been stealing then buying them once she could just for shits and giggles for years.

"Can you excuse me?" Shona said to her client, walking to the front. She kicked the back of Marilyn's chair who yelled, "Huh?" then

"Oh, hey. How can I help you? You have an appointment?" realizing someone had walked in.

"Hi, and no I don't. I'm new in the neighborhood and decided to stop by. Finding a hairdresser is so stressful," the woman said, then laughed. "I'm London."

She batted her eyes, staring at Shona who's presence exuded confidence. She was definitely eye candy with a touch of hood to her.

"Pleasure to meet you, London. I'm Shona. Excuse my receptionist, Marilyn. It's still early."

Marilyn rubbed the back of her neck, feeling the heat from Shona's body. She was a college kid just trying to earn a few bucks. She was cheap, a clear sign Shona got what she paid for.

"So, you're the owner?" the woman said, sounding more like a question. "Interesting."

"Why is that interesting?" Shona asked, putting on a fake smile before she went off on her.

"No reason," London told her, looking around.

The woman was in awe. She figured whoever had decorated this place had to have a degree in interior design. It was edgy, yet chic. The tiles, chair, and washing bins all a soft pink and eggshell color.

"Well, I want her," she said to Marilyn, pointing at Remy who was chatting away on her cell. "Can you check her availability? And money is never a problem. I can tell you're good, really good."

"Me?" Remy asked her, catching London's eyes that looked her way. Remy took one look at the woman and damn near started to twerk.

"Oh?" Shona said, then smiled, wondering what that was about.

Every cosmetologist in there could hold their weight, but clearly Remy wasn't the one many came to The Palace to see first. Shona was no hater, though. She was just as enthused as everyone else, while Remy rambled on excitedly about her new potential client.

"Girl, some rich bitch done came in here and want me to do her hair," Remy tried to whisper. "You remember that bag I was telling you about? Hoe, the grey, gator-skinned Dooney and Burke one with the pink leather straps? Yassss, bitch. That one!"

London laughed, unsure as to why Remy was really here when she didn't seem to care about first impressions. She did, however, fit perfectly into her plan. She smiled at her while Remy only confirmed all the more what she knew and what she needed—she was the underdog.

All underdogs had talent, but this one was messy with hers.

Bingo, London thought and smiled.

"Oh, yes. Book me with her." It didn't hurt that Remy look like she could stand to have a high end client, looking at the cheap bundle of weave her current client was getting sewn into her head.

"What about next Saturday at ten in the morning? Does that work?"

"It's perfect. Shona, it's been a pleasure to meet you. And Remy, you have any business cards?"

"Ugh, hold on. She asking for business cards. All interrupting me, I forgot what I was even saying." Remy then looked up and said, "Naw, boo. Not today. Find me on Facebook though."

Chaney and Shona laughed, wondering if she went with Remy because she could walk all over her or would kiss her ass, but clearly she chose wrong.

"Oh, okay. What's your name so I can?" London finally asked her smiling, although she looked to be in pain. She wasn't sure how much of this low class bitch she could stomach, watching Shona smile and chuckle lowly.

"Remy. You know, like the drink? Remy Dat Bitch on Facebook. That's my page name," she said, like she was proud of herself.

"Oh, I will. Okay, Remy. See you next Saturday." London then took off just as quietly and smoothly as she did coming in.

Once the door closed, Shona got a strange feeling about this woman. But one thing she said that had gotten her attention. If money was not a problem for her, it damn sure wasn't a problem for Shona.

"Make a note I'm charging her ass double for anything she gets. I will show her just how interesting I am. Of all the spots in the Miami, she came here. So yeah, we're charging her for being a bitch," she snickered.

Marilyn covered her mouth and laughed, "Boss lady, that's mean."

"No, what's mean is me firing you because I expected more than substandard customer service skills. Give me these," Shona told her, taking her headphones. "Write down what I said and now."

When she turned around to go back to her client, she caught Chaney, Shelby and Remy all staring and smiling. "What?" she asked them, turning her lip up.

"Nothing," Shelby said, dropping her head like she was clueless.

"Boss lady, you did real good, but she was acting like she was all that. I liked how you handled her though," Remy said, kissing her ass. "I ain't scared of you like these two, but you my bitch. Ayeeee," she sang, walking up and high-fiving her.

"You're silly," Shona shot back, laughing.

"I'll be that," Remy replied, sticking out her tough and giggling.

Things weren't perfect in her world, but they could be worse. She no longer had the crew, but she somehow created a new dysfunctional family of misguided women. All she needed was Kaleela back and then she would feel somewhat complete.

CHAPTER THIRTEEN

"Your honor, my client Jamal Brooks has had a clean record until this incident. He's a role model in his community, held down a part-time job all throughout high school to help his mother care for his five younger siblings," X started out, his eyes landing gently on each juror. Even without trying, the woman seemed to be in awe of him. Still, this was business and he didn't come play.

"Since he's been a college student, he's maintained a 3.0 GPA. This incident was not an incident. It was two consenting people who agreed to have sex. We do know what consent is, don't we?" he asked and a gasp was heard followed by a chuckle from the floor.

He held a stone face, trying to ignore anything that could influence the appeal he was making. Ace told him by now he should be used to it. He was. He just didn't like it. If he wanted to pick up a bitch, it wouldn't be in the a trial or courtroom.

"Objection, your honor."

"What grounds?" Judge Huggins said, used to the reaction X got now. He even tried getting off the case himself, but couldn't just so he wouldn't have to chastise grown women.

"What he said!" the prosecuting attorney spat, standing up. With a stern look, he got himself together. "What I meant was there were more than two of them involved. How could that be consensual?" His name was Stewart Slutsky, a high-profile attorney winning many controversial cases, but even X intimidated him.

"Overruled. Clearly you know more than two people can be involved in the act that he speaks of," Judge Higgins said, cutting his eyes his way before he looked at X. "And you, watch it."

"Yes, your honor," X said, loosening up his tie.

"Now, Mr. West? Were more than two?"

"Your honor, unless we are trying all defendants right now, this trial speaks to Jamal. I have presented clear evidence that his client, Wendy Rodgers, initiated meeting up with my client. Even after multiple times of him turning her down."

Looking at the jury with seven women and five men, he was still winning but he wanted them to set his client free because it was the truth. Not because of how he moved about and looked in the courtroom. This wasn't a dick-slinging contest either as the men grunted or smirked his way.

"If he were your son who went off to college and worked hard, often known to have many women pursuing him, imagine what you would say to him. Let's be honest?" X said, making sure to give his attention went to the male jurors. "Fathers encourage their sons to sow their royal oats when they are young. Not to settle down so soon while mothers just ask them to not lie to those girls."

"I feel like we're in church," Stuart mumbled, shaking his head.

"The prosecution has shown you nothing but two consenting adults, and once he finally agreed to meet up with her, the two had sex. No more, no less. Everything after that is Miss Rodger's bruised ego of him not wanting more after that." He stopped and turned to the plaintiff.

"Don't," Stuart said, standing up and slapping the table.

"Counsel, to the bench *now*," Judge Higgins demanded, leaning on one elbow as he wagged them over with one finger.

"You deserve better," was all X said to her lowly before he followed the other counsel to the judge's bench.

She wiped a tear, dropping her head. Everything he said was true. She only wanted attention, often feeling overlooked when compared to her older sister who excelled at everything. She was her sister's shadow, often coming in second.

This was the first time in her life she actually had her parents' undivided attention all behind a fake rape case. She glanced at Jamal, who looked like he was carrying the world on his shoulders. She felt awful, coming to the realization that he didn't deserve this. She agreed to sex, even asking his friends to come along.

"I ought to fine the both of you," Judge Higgins told them. "You, for playing church and you for acting a fool in my courtroom."

"But—"

"Counsel," Judge Higgins warned Mr. Slutsky. "Look at your client. She's falling a part. She's in love with that boy."

X looked back, watching her stare at Jamal who sat shaking as he fought back tears. He felt for her, but he's loyalty and obligation was to his client and his client only.

"Mr. Slutsky," she called out, shocking the entire room. Gasps and whispers could be heard. "May I speak?"

"Get over there now," Judge Higgins told him. "Miss Rodgers, please wait for counsel," he urged her.

Once he did, she leaned over and whispered in her attorney's ear. X could tell whatever she said made him uncomfortable, his face turning red. He asked her something and she shook her head no, grabbing a napkin in front of her as tears fell.

"Your honor," he finally said, now loosening his own tie. "May counsel approach the bench again?"

X looked back at Jamal and smiled. He didn't know what was said, but it had Mr. Slutsky flustered. X stood there waiting patiently, yet eager to celebrate. He was hoping his client and the plaintiff could one day make amends, but all he wanted now was for Jamal's charges to be dropped.

"Alright, let's hear it, Mr. Slutsky."

"My client has asked that we put on the record that she was not completely truthful."

"What part, counsel?"

He cleared his throat. "All of it."

"What does that mean, counsel? And be very clear when you

answer before I make a decision that will have you in court with her on the other side."

"She only solicited Jamal, but went along with it when she came over and his friends were there. He even asked her to leave, but she didn't," he said, his voice trailing off. "They started drinking and the rest is…well, you know the rest."

"Yes," X celebrated under his breath until Judge Huggins gave him a look. "Sorry, your honor."

"Mr. Slutsky, it is unfortunate this young man had to go through this. I know as her counsel, you have done everything to represent your client. While I certainly understand the struggles young people go through, it does not give them a right to destroy someone else's life.

The charges shall be dismissed, but make no mistake about it, your client may be back in my courtroom at a later date. My concern right now, however, is letting Mr. Brooks go."

"I understand, your honor."

"You better. And Mr. West?"

"Yes, your honor," he said all too quickly, dropping his smile.

"Thank God she had a conscience. Now get out of here before I hold all of these female jurors in contempt of court." X looked over and at least two were fanning themselves. "Now both take your seats."

As soon as they did, the whispers slowly came to halt as the judge cleared his throat.

"It has come to my attention that Miss Rodgers recalls the night of the incident a little differently. As such, the charges against Jamal Brooks will be dismissed. I so order on this day. Mr. Brooks, my apologies to you and your family. I will be sure to follow up with the university to ensure your privileges are reinstated fully."

"Thank you, your honor," Jamal said, breaking down crying as X leaned over and hugged him.

"Miss Brooks, today could be a sad day for you but I would like to say for now that it's a time to truly look inside of yourself. We all may not like everything about ourselves, but we should all love ourselves no matter what. You have a wonderful mother and father.

I have heard them speak very passionately about you. I challenge you all to seek family counseling, but even if that does not occur, you should go and get the help you need. Court is now adjourned." Hitting his gavel, the bailiff then said, "All rise."

X stood up and shook Jamal's hand. "Now, you owe me."

Jamal didn't know what that meant, but he didn't care. He had spent a year in the county jail. He was ready to go home and spend some time with his family.

His mother, looking worn and tired, walked up to her son and grabbed his face. "Baby, God is good. Didn't I tell you?"

"Yes, ma'am," he replied, getting choked up all over again. He wailed like a big baby, holding on to his mother. His father, although not around like he should be, joined them. X overheard him apologizing to his son, agreeing to be around more.

X became somewhat teary-eyed but kept his composure. He wished there was some way he and his father could finally find a common ground and co-exist in love. He looked up and caught who he thought was his father, walking out of the courtroom.

"Naw, I'm tripping," he said to himself. He looked back at Jamal who was now hugging his father. "Mr. Brooks, I told your son he owes me but all I really want him to do is to never forget where he came from. This world comes with a lot of desirable things that can get in our way," X said to Jamal's father.

"He won't because we both are going to do this together, Mr. West. I promise. Every single dime Maybelle owes you will be paid."

"No, we're good," he said, holding up his hand. "What my office has received is enough. Just stick around because no matter how old we get, a black man will always need his father."

Shaking hands with other attorneys in the room, X slipped down the hallway avoiding the reporters outside. He wasn't into public interviews, only appearing at a press conference if it benefitted his clients.

Walking into the parking garage, he unlocked his Benz and threw his briefcase in the trunk. He pulled his cell out and saw he had quite a few missed calls. They were from his mother, Ace, Tooley, and even his father.

Choosing to call Ace back first, X dialed him back. "What's up, Ace? I was in court. All y'all calling me. Which one of y'all asses won the lotto?"

"Shit, I wish one of us unlucky bitches did," he said, his voice low as he walked away to a quieter area as his voice got clearer. "I need you to come to Baptist Hospital."

"Why? Milky Way has finally flipped on you, slap your ass up good? I told you to stop messing around with them strippers." Ace hadn't really seen Milky Way since Gabby came home to his place. No one even knew he had a houseguest at this point, and for now, he was keeping it that way.

"I wish it was that," he said, taking a deep breath and exhaling. "It's Reagan. She was in an accident. She's hanging in there, but bruh, it don't look good."

Everything in front of him slowed down, the air in his body suspended in his lungs. X couldn't believe what he had just heard. Reagan, to his knowledge, wasn't even driving anymore. She hadn't in months.

He dropped his cell, taking off with no regard for his own life. If Reagan died, he would feel guilty. As of late, he'd spent most of his time in the office working hard to save others, but couldn't save his own sister.

Just when things were starting to look good in his life, no longer worrying about a bitch or pussy, this happened.

CHAPTER FOURTEEN

"Hi, my name is Kaleela Bradley and I am an alcoholic."

"Hi, Kaleela," the others said, greeting her with smiling faces. Today was her last there and the first day of the rest of her life. She had completed her first sixty days of sobriety, allowing her to go home and start her journey attending outpatient treatment.

It was hard, but she turned down visits from Shona and made her promise not to tell anyone where she was. She looked around and saw new faces she would now call family.

Just like Shona seeing the girls at the shop as her new family, Kaleela somehow found a family, too. She smiled, watching the slight discomfort on her sister's face as she sat two seats over from Chico.

Still, no matter what, in her eyes, he had saved both of their lives. She just prayed her sister would get it together so both of them could happy for her, even if his wife was sitting there too. If asked, Shona would say she was very happy for him. But she couldn't lie. It just felt strange sharing the same space with the woman she had looked at for years as her enemy. The woman that stood in between her fate and her happily forever after.

"I am happy to say that today I have sixty days clean and sober." A few shouted yes while others clapped, making her feel really good. "To be honest, I can't remember the last time I went more than a day or two without drinking since I was like fourteen.

I grew up fast and lived hard. Drinking and getting high were like getting up, washing my face and brushing my teeth. It wasn't until my sister, with her mean ass—" she said, pointing at Shona. "—got me right. I swear I love her aggy as—I mean self," Kaleela said, trying to act civilize like Shona raised her to be as much as she could.

"Sheesh," Shona mumbled, scooting down with one hand over her face.

"Don't hide now," she said, calling her out. "She's the one over there who's covering her face, trying to disown me." The room laughed, someone behind her patting Shona on the shoulder. She was embarrassed, but happy at the same time.

She waved at a few who looked her way. She hated attention no matter what others thought, urging Kaleela with stretched eyes to keep going.

"Yeah, well, Shona talks plenty of sh—stuff. See, I caught myself again. This AA is really working."

Everyone chimed in from where they sat, clapping their hands. Kaleela was always quite the funny and charming one, not losing her touch. Even when she wasn't trying. Shona was proud of her holding her own up there, being responsible.

"I guess it was just something about this time that let me know if I didn't choose this route, I would go on in life alone without her." Kaleela stopped after she said that, pinching her eyes as she tried to hold back the tears.

"You can do it, K baby. We got you. Crew for life," Chico shouted, causing her to laugh.

"It's that crew mess that got me wild, yo. Y'all don't listen to him. Everything I know, he taught me." People started laughing and clapping, looking at him while he smiled. "But one thing he taught me that even he don't know is that it's okay to mess up. You just can't keep messing up. Like he's seen me grow. I've see him grow too and I'm proud to see him doing the right thing."

Myriah leaned over and rubbed his forearm, kissing his cheek. Shona took a peek, seeing the love in his wife's eyes for him. For the first time, she finally believed that Chico had chosen the right one. She didn't hate it. She just wanted it too.

Without overthinking it, Shona reached over, extending her hand to Myriah. She looked stunned at first, but slowly accepted the gesture. They shook, saying no words but it was clear in that moment that everyone was moving on.

"Now, since this is not only my day, I need to wrap it up. Besides, I get to eat some real food later on. My bro and his wife I heard hooked me up," she said, rubbing her hands with her tongue out.

"Ugh, ma'am," Shona told her, forcing her to close it shut.

"Anyway," she said, squinting her way as she waved her off. She was going to have to remind Shona she wasn't a kid later on, but for now, she would let her make it. "I will end this by saying to my peers, if I can do it, you can do it too. I still have a ways to go, but my mind is clearer now. I can wake up and actually focus, actually make better decisions... I hope." They all laughed when someone shouted, "Ammmmen!"

"A preacher I'm not," Kaleela said quickly, looking around. The room got a kick out of that, especially her roommate who was snorting when she giggled. She always did. It was that snort that got Kaleela's attention. She could tell her roomie was used to the nice shit, but came in with a bad attitude.

One night she tried Kaleela and a quick drop kick but by a swift hand underneath her feet, let her know that Kaleela's wheelchair wasn't a sign she couldn't handle herself or others, for that matter. They got into a scuffle, surprising Kaleela that she could hang.

Ever since then, they were thick as thieves, her roommate having one more month to go. She had already done a few weeks in the hospital, and now rehab as a condition in lieu of jail for her fourth DUI.

Kaleela caught her tearing up, quickly going to her when it was over. while Shona sat quietly, thanking God her sister was still alive. When the graduation was over, Kaleela left to go get her things, leaving Shona all alone with Chico and his wife.

"So, how far along are you?" Shona asked, deciding to just break the ice and be mature. Myriah, who was expecting, grinned so hard as she rubbed her small, yet firm belly. Being petite, she always carried small, but still seemed to have large babies.

"Almost five months now," she said, sipping some punch. Myriah looked good, but she always did. Shona even noticed the baby had made her hair longer and thicker. She could even tell how healthy it was as it moved with ease from the slightest move. "I think this is it. Ishmael's practically grown, heading off to college soon. And I feel so old and fat," she said, laughing nervously. "I better stop since this will be baby number four. I swear this has to be it."

"Girl, fat where?" Shona spat, waving her hand at her. "You look great."

"That's what I'm talking about," Chico chimed in, kissing his wife lovingly on the forehead as he walked up. "Carrying my babies can't never make her fat. Just juicy."

"Oh boy, stop it," Myriah said, lightly pushing him off of her.

Chico eyed Shona, wanting to reach out for a hug. It didn't hurt she was fine as hell, even more than before dressed professionally yet elegantly in a pair of slacks and top that swooped lowly down her back.

It almost hurt him to be so close, but the woman before him now wasn't playing any games. She was holding her own and he couldn't do nothing but respect that.

He was still happy with his decision though. His own wife was looking good herself, rocking a black dress that loosely hung over her belly along with a diamond choker that matched her diamond stiletto heels.

Shona dropped her head, feeling the need to say something Kaleela's speech inspired. Chico had always been there. No matter what she chose to believe, he never made her his one and only. She just wanted him too. Hell, even Myriah played the side bitch. So, in essence, he had fucked them both over. She just ended up with his son and the rest was history from there.

So she did the next shocking thing for the evening, quickly saying, "I'm sorry, Myriah. I truly am."

Her voice had pain in it, the kind that sunk in deeply, followed by her eyes. They were sad, even though she tried to hide it. Yet, Myriah knew she was sincere, taking a deep breath as she registered what she had heard.

Even she knew it took two to play, especially after she played two friends for many years back in the day. It was Chico and his best friend, Keyz. Today, they were all cool now. Hell, in laws since Keyz married Myriah's younger sister, Iyana. If they could get over all of that dark history, Myriah figured why can't she and Shona.

She too took notice of how well put together Shona was, wearing charcoal grey slacks and a pale pink, sexy shirt that matched her pale pink Jimmy Choo shoes. Her makeup was flawless, complementing her hair that was now streaked with a soft, hot pink highlight in her blondish hair. It wasn't overbearing either, barely covering two to three areas throughout her thick bob.

Myriah pursed her lips, raising her cup up to her mouth as she took another a sip of punch. "I accept. I honestly do. Maybe one day—"

"Don't push it," Shona jumped in and said, touching her shoulder. "I'm still me. You're safe, but that man of yours can still catch these hands or a few hot ass bullets." They both laughed as he smirked, shaking his head but Shona was serious.

"Ugh—"

"Girl, I'm kidding," Shona laughed as she cut her off. She then opened her arms as she welcomed Myriah her way with a hug. She closed her eyes, not wanting to see Chico's face. The heart wanted what it wanted, but hers could want his. So she couldn't even look his way right now. Not when she was emotional.

As the two women chatted, he finally felt some relief. Honestly, he wasn't surprised they were talking. He went in today, hoping they all could. Once he heard on the street what had happened to Kaleela, he visited the facility one day, leaving her a letter.

He apologized for not setting the best example for her and hurting her and her sister. Each week, they wrote back and forth and true to his word, he showed up with his wife in tow. Shona forgiving him would be all he needed to really move on. Christmas morning just didn't leave him feeling so good, but this was making him feel better.

"Shona," he said, smiling. He knew not to call her Shonasia. That was their thing and they were no longer "a thing". "Thank you."

"No problem," she said, turning away to clear her throat.

"Baby, everything's alright?" he asked his wife, deciding to leave it right there. The Shona he knew was probably carrying her hit. He damn sure was and he knew she wasn't afraid to use it.

"Of course it is," she said, walking and standing next to Shona. "It's you that can still catch her hands, like she said."

Shona busted out laughing, clapping her hands so loud that Kaleela sped over there feeling embarrassed.

"Shona, are you drinking?" she grunted lowly with a scowl on her face. "Man, why she gotta be so loud?' she asked Chico, sucking her teeth.

"Oh, shut up. As many times as you have embarrassed me? You better go roll your ass on back from wherever you came from."

Myriah couldn't help it, almost spitting out her juice. "Oh my."

"You're sober now. I promise you will feel everything I throw your way, K baby. Showing your ass now."

They all laughed while Kaleela mean mugged her, as her roommate appeared with a man. A handsome one at that, making Shona's eyes stretched wide open.

"Anyway. Shona, this is my roomie, my homegirl, Reagan. Reagan, this is my big head sister Shona. She thinks she's my mama."

"I am her mother. Don't I look fabulous?" she said, in her proper voice trying to ignore X who didn't seem to even look her way. She was hoping he didn't so she could get out of there. She felt bad after she did him that way that night. Especially when she found out it was he that got Kaleela's truck back to their house.

X's eyes finally stopped wandering, landing on Kaleela and then Shona. *Dang, this is shorty from the strip club*, he said to himself. He remembered when she tried to shit on him in front of his boys, unsure of how he felt about her now.

Then he fixed his eyes on Kaleela who just shook her head. She didn't remember all the details, but she was hoping his homeboy who she fucked up wasn't there. Shona, quickly turned away, hoping he would speak and leave.

He returned his attention to Kaleela who had her own attitude. He could tell she definitely knew who he was.

"What's up?" he said, grinning.

"Nothing, what's up?" When she did, she gave him that look like she was ready to fight. He dismissed that look with a friendly smirk, giving his attention to Shona. The longer he stared, the more he realized she mesmerized him.

"Look, I don't know you like that, but staring is rude."

"And? So is not speaking," he told her, chuckling as her skin flushed with warm, red undertones.

"Whatever," she mumbled. "Just relax with that staring shit."

"Damn right," Kaleela said, rolling closer his way. Reagan stood by laughing, floored. She would never put two and two together, but now she remembered X mentioning some chick at a strip club hitting Tooley. The wheelchair went right over her head, but this had to be fate.

X smiled, watching how Kaleela came at him, wearing a light blue Nike t-shirt, dark blue Coach sneakers, and light blue jeans almost two sizes too big.

"Anyway, good evening. I'm Xander."

Kaleela looked at it and smirked, wishing she had her 9-millimeter in her hand. Kaleela wasn't drunk now, so she would not only remember, but enjoy popping him now for talking shit. By then, Shona had taken off.

"You said Xander?" Chico asked, taking a gulp of his juice. He'd been watching the whole time, ready to bust X in his mouth. He knew Shona, so something had to be up with the way she cleared it.

"Well, we call him X, but Xander is his real name," Reagan said, feeling the tension as she smiled. She shook Chico and Myriah's hand, while X gave them his back.

By now, he had zoned out, watching Shona across the room as she playfully laughed and chatted with a few others she'd gotten to know in the family Al Anon support group. They too would forever be family, since their family members had the same struggle.

Even though Reagan had only been there a month, the only thing Kaleela talked about was her roommate who was loud and ghetto. X couldn't agree more, laughing that she was the same female who's sister he honestly couldn't stop thinking about.

Shona caught him looking, but did her best to act interested in whatever these people were talking about, hoping he'd go on about his business. She wasn't ready to apologize to him and she definitely knew the look he was wearing. He wanted to fuck and she wasn't having it.

As she noticed him coming her way, she was about to head to the restroom, but stopped. Tonight was Kaleela's night, so she decided to play nice. Especially since Kaleela and his sister were pretty cool. Chances are, Reagan would come around. So she figured being nice tonight was her way of supporting her sister's new friend. And a friend Kaleela didn't seem too interesting in having sex with although Reagan was extremely beautiful.

"Excuse me, but I'm X, Reagan's brother," he said, reaching for her hand. Reagan bent down and nudged Kaleela, whispering in her ear as they stared on.

"Shonasia," she said, surprising even Myriah who watched Shona give him a broad smile. She couldn't hate on her at all. Shona was stunning, looking at Chico who seemed to be fuming. "But they call me Shona."

"Oh oh, she's never friendly. The only man she's even let get close to her is... never mind," Kaleela said to Reagan, subtly tossing her head at Chico.

"Whew," was all Reagan said, seeing how fine Chico was. "The girl does have good taste."

"Well, he ain't getting that. Shona aint' fucking with your brother. Ain't he a pig?" Kaleela said, shaking her head.

"Hoe, no. My brother is a lawyer," she snapped.

"Shit, same thing. Now let me get over there before Shona lose her shit. I know my sister.

"No, let him watch," Reagan suggested, referring to Chico. "She's a single woman and your boy over there is married, right?"

"Pretty much," Kaleela replied, hoping they would behave themselves.

Reagan didn't know all the details but she figured this was Shona's one time to prove she was that bitch. She enjoyed watching Chico watch her brother make his move. She hated Avery, and since Kaleela was her girl now, she thought it would be cute if their siblings linked up. Falling back, Kaleela sat there hoping Reagan was right.

"X, is it?" Shona said, looking at his hand. "What, you forgot about the other letters in the alphabet? And that this is still my hand."

"Cute. That was cute and it's my hand for now," he told her, still holding on to it as she laughed lowly, dropping her head.

Shona was thoroughly impressed with how he cleaned up, dressed in a tan Italian suit and tan Stacey Adams shoes. His cologne was intoxicating too, causing her head to swim.

And his lips were like lips she wanted planted on and inside of her center. She quickly shook it off, hoping he didn't catch her slipping, getting caught up in how he had pulled her in that quickly. It didn't matter though. She pulled him in that quickly, too.

X chuckled to himself, remembering that slick mouth she had that night that somehow had abandoned her. But what hadn't were her thighs, hips, and ass in those charcoal slacks. Her body alone had him ready to break all kinds of rules it was so sickening.

He couldn't believe Reagan's addiction brought not only the crazy girl back that whipped Tooley's ass, but the one he'd couldn't keep his mind off of since that night they crossed each other's paths.

"I'm..." she said at a loss for words, which was new for her.

"Fucking stunning," X said, finishing her sentence because to him, she was. He knew he overstepped, wanting to give her some time to realize he was about to be all up in her space. He usually didn't chase, but he could tell, she would make it fun once that mean streak she owned reappeared. He needed fun and a woman that wouldn't just give in to him was exactly that.

"Thank you, X," she replied, a sly grin on her face. She was too cute, lightly swiping a strand of her out of her face as he reduced the space the between them. "So are you."

They both laughed at that when she did. Hearing a woman compliment his looks in that way wasn't new, but it felt better than good coming from her.

"I guess I am a pretty motherfucker."

"Oh God," she said, shaking her head.

"Well, super star, it's been a pleasure," he said, ending the high he'd just too her on. She wasn't sure if she was relieved or upset, stopping him.

"Wait. Why super—"

She couldn't even finish when he quickly bent down and kissed her just short of her mouth.

"Because you make a nigga feel like he's on top of the world. Hell, and I don't even know you like that." He was so close, so bold, so confident, never once moving as she gulped. "To do that, you must have some super powers or something."

"O—okay," she stuttered, then shook her head like she couldn't believe what had just happened with a smile. Kaleela was shocked, ready for Shona to kick some ass when X go that close, but she stumped it seemed. Even Chico was taken aback with a stranger all in her personal space.

Shona took a deep breath, making X feel like his job was done when she did. He'd planted the seed of connection, so all he had to do is wait. As she lightly touched where his lips landed without realizing she had, he turned around to the others to bid them a good night.

"Get my number from Reagan," he told Shona.

"Get mine and you know how," she said laughing, feeling Chico's eyes bore into her face. She ignored it, chewing on the left side of her bottom lip.

"I will. And it was a pleasure meeting all of you."

He nodded at Chico before he reached for Myriah's hand, kissing it softly. "You're beautiful, too."

He winked his eye, waiting for Chico to say some shit that would get him fucked up tonight, but he didn't. X was sure he was probably the reason these two women had obvious tension, watching him twitch when Myriah gasped lightly then smiled.

"Thank you," Myriah as Chico chewed the inside of jaw.

"Reagan, walk me out, baby girl."

Shona's panties were noticeably moist as she squirmed just a little. She looked down at Kaleela who had a mischievous grin on her face. She had never seen a man shut her sister up and smile at the same time. Definitely not a man she'd only had a few encounters with, eyeing her suspiciously.

Kaleela knew that look on her sister's face, seeing it in plenty of bitch's faces she'd fucked over the years once she stepped to them. She then looked at Chico, trying to find the quickest way to get her sister out of there. No way was she letting her night be ruined by their old bullshit.

"A'ight, bro. I'm leaving with y'all. She's going to head on back home," she said, speaking for Shona who looked confused.

"Wait, you're not coming over to eat after all the food I cooked?" Myriah asked.

Before their little apology session, she made sure to go all out cooking everything from fried chicken, a honey baked ham to roast beef for meats. Then candied yams, collard greens, cornbread soufflé, potato salad, and a German chocolate cake from scratch. She wasn't being messy, but she wasn't about to make her question why he chose her. She was that girl in and outside of the bedroom.

Shona wanted to curse Kaleela out, but she didn't, deciding it was a good time to leave.

"Uh, uh. No, I'm tired," Shona lied, now feeling warm. *What the hell is wrong with me*, she asked herself but she knew.

What was wrong was Xander West or X.

CHAPTER FIFTEEN

The summer had come and Gabby had grown bored. It had been about three months now. All of that chemistry she felt at the hospital with Ace had gone right out the door once he took her home. Ace, the perfect gentleman, gave her his master bedroom, moving on the other side of the house.

She couldn't understand why a single man needed a four-bed/three bath home but had it decorated as if an entire family lived there. She'd spend hours going from room to room, imagining what she would do differently if it were home to decorate. It wasn't bad, but it definitely needed a softer, feminine touch.

When she wasn't alone snooping, Gabby actually was being productive, now an online student working on a master' s degree in social work. It was one of the goals she and her therapist discussed as something she felt could help her healing process. It also would allow her to work with other domestic violence victims while interning before she landed a job in that field.

She had even dropped twenty pounds, working out on the exercise equipment he had in one of the rooms, too. One day she went in there to be nosy like always, and he'd caught her. Instead of chastising her, he challenged her to get on the treadmill for twenty minutes. Soon twenty turned into thirty and she was doing now up to an hour at least four times a week.

She still hadn't called her family, afraid Tyson might have reached out, and she barely left the house unless she was with Ace. He'd done a great job introducing her to his closest friends, but she was just as lonely as she was before since it stopped right there.

Looking at the time, she was glad she had just finished dinner. Ace never required her to do anything, even clean up since he had a maid come a few times a week, but Gabby still did her part and more. And since she liked to cook, a daily hot meal it was.

One day while searching online, an ad got her interest. It was for a hair salon that was looking for a nail technician. Often made to hide her beauty, Gabby learned how to do her own manicure and pedicure. She'd even snuck and took classes, becoming a certified nail technician, but never did anything with it.

As soon as he walked in, she heard Ace mumbling under his breath as he smelled the dinner she made. She was so caught up in the help wanted ad, she didn't even know he'd walked in.

"She did it again," Ace said to himself, inhaling something that was spicy coming from the kitchen. He loved spicy food. She knew that, too, making him want to cross that line. He'd been fighting for months not to. He was beyond attracted to her, but he knew getting over one man wasn't about getting underneath another one.

"Gabby, where are you?" While he waited for her to respond, he grabbed the mail, looking through it before he took his keys and cell phone out of his pocket.

He had to go back out in a few hours, but he tried to spend at least an hour or two with her on those days.

She slipped into the living room, watching him talk under his breath. She could smell his cologne all the way over there from the other side of the room, wishing they were a couple so she could greet him properly. She'd been practicing too, parading around in a shirt of his when she was home alone just to smell him on her body.

"Hey," she said, not moving from where she was. She was trying to see what kind of mood he was in, something she often did when it came to Tyson.

"Hey," he said, turning around and smiling. She was glad too since he already told her she didn't have to cook.

"Why did you cook again, Gabby?"

There is it, she said to herself, shrinking inside. He did too, quickly changing his approach. He wasn't chastising her, but he knew the smallest thing could make her feel like she was. "I'm just saying, Gabriela. We have tons of food in there from last night and the night before."

She dropped her eyes, upset that she disappointed him.

"Gabriela?" he said, this time softer, catching her attention. He was the only one that called her that and not all the time. But when he did, she liked it. It made her feel like a princess, a slim and cute on like in a Disney movie even though she was far from slim.

He silently cursed himself, walked up to her and lifting up her chin.

"What do I like to see from you whenever we talk?" Ace asked her, his voice very soft as he remembered to be non-threatening.

She smiled, admiring his smooth, dark skin against his white teeth. His hair, = growing out some, was starting to curl. She liked it though. It him a softer, boyish look, but what didn't look boyish was his body. No, Ace's body was toned and thick. Signs of a man who took great care of his body. She wanted to touch it, but was afraid she might be rejected.

"My eyes?" she asked, already knowing the answer.

He stroked the side of her face, fighting what he really wanted to do as she subconsciously leaned into his hand.

"Hell yeah," he said with a smile. He wanted to kiss her so bad, falling hard without even trying to. Gabby was perfect, even in all of her self proclaimed imperfections. He didn't give a damn about her weight either, mad each time she spoke on it.

He wanted her to tell how just how much it tortured him to not touch her, to fuck her, to make her his own. Some nights, he'd hit up a random chick or Milky Way before coming home just so he could ignore her. But it was getting harder and harder, especially after the last time he called Milky Way her name.

He laid his nose on top of her head, running his fingers up the nape of her neck. His laced her hair around his fingers and he gently pulled her head back until their eyes met. He heard her gasp, her breath cascading down his face and neck. He smelled that funny cotton candy smell that always seemed to find its way leaping off her skin.

"I'm sorry for seeming ungrateful," he whispered, lifting her by her chin once more. "I just want you to know you're not here to be my maid. You're here to heal and shit, do whatever the fuck you want to do."

A light went off, causing her to smile. She wasn't sure if it was the best idea, but it was an idea nonetheless.

"What?" he said, his smile matching hers.

"I could do something else, you know. Like a find a little job," she said just above a whisper.

"A job?" he repeated, frowning. "I'm not sure about that. Where Gabby? I can find you a volunteer spot or something, but..." he said and paused, shaking his head. "I don't know."

He had his eyes on Tyson, but he hadn't touched him yet. From the looks of it, he was doing badly but his time was coming. It was all about timing, so Gabby wasn't quite out of the woods just yet.

"Never mind," she mumbled, dropping her head.

"Look," he said, pulling her down on his lap. "Tell me about this job."

"Yeah?" she said, her eyes lightening up.

"Yes, Gabriela." She wanted to squeal, enjoying whenever her government name rolled off of his tongue. "Show me."

She quickly reached for her laptop, and went to the page. "Look, and the area is in a very nice neighborhood."

"The Palace," he said under his breath. "Hmmm, let me look into it and see who's the owner. I can do that tomorrow. Is that too late?" he asked, watching her grin like a little kid.

"No, that's perfect," she said, jumping up. "It's dinner time."

Ace was thinking he'd rather eat her, but smiled and replied, "Dinner sounds good, Gabriela. Damn good."

Slowly walking backwards, Gabby couldn't believe her luck was turning around. In a little less than a six months, she'd lost at least thirty pounds, started counseling and school and was now about to get a new job. She also had given her heart to a man that didn't even know he had it.

Damn, she sure wished he did know. She gladly let him have her for dinner just like he wanted to.

CHAPTER SIXTEEN

"He—hello, is anyone here?" Gabby asked, peeking her head inside of The Palace. Ace gave her the go ahead to check it out, but she couldn't help but notice the unmarked car that followed her that was sitting outside.

Gabby stood there, watching Shona sing and dance to music only she could hear with headphones in her ears. From the words she caught in between mumbles, it sounded like Ciara's "Level Up" as she did a cute two-step.

Gabby already liked her, watching her dance in a boyfriend-style jean overall with a white tank top and low-top, hot pink Converse. Her hair, a cherry cola bob with pink highlights, loosely swung back and forth as she swept the floor to the beat.

Once Shona turned around, she jumped and screamed, dropping the broom. Gabby, startled by her outburst, started screaming, too. As they both screamed, Kaleela rolled out from the back with her nine, swinging it left and right between the two of them.

"Uh, uh, uh! Oh my God! I'm so sorry! I—I'm Gabby!" she apologized, grabbing her chest trying to catch her breath. "I—I saw the ad. It was for a nail technician."

Shona, taking deep breaths, cursed silently. She was more upset with herself for leaving the front door unlocked. It didn't matter that they were in a nice area. She knew better. She quickly walked past Gabby, closing and locking the front door.

"Abby or whatever your name is, you better talk sooner around here or your chest will be leaking," Kaleela warned her, tucking her heat back in her ankle strap.

"Kaleela," Shona fussed, giving her the eye.

"Shit, what? You too. Better be glad I'm practicing this sobriety thing," she shot back, whipping her wheelchair around as she headed back to the office.

Shona wasn't sure what was up with Kaleela. Things had been good but for the past few days since she'd been home, she'd been grouchy. She told her to ease back into things but truthfully, her own head was all over the place thinking of X.

"I'm so sorry, I really am. My sister shouldn't have done that, but you did sort of sneak up on us. She honestly meant no harm," Shona told her, watching Gabby who looked like she wanted to run. She wasn't sure who toted a gun and rode in a wheelchair acting like that, but her mind was blown.

Instead of responding right away, Gabby took a moment to gain her bearings. She rubbed her hands up and down her distressed jeans, smiling nervously. She wasn't sure what to say next.

Shona took notice of how the jeans nicely hugged her full figure, wearing a yellow, one shoulder sheer top and cami that hung over her hips with some skinny jeans. The shoulder exposed an exotic butterfly tattoo on the right shoulder. Her hair, a long Peruvian weave, made Shona want to shout "bitch" it looked that good. It was full of long, wavy curls hung loosely over one shoulder. She finished her look off wearing six-inch heels as if she had on a pair of Nikes, standing with ease.

"Look, it's fine," Gabby finally spoke, her voice clearly still shaky. "I was just trying to see if the job was still open. But when I saw you singing and sweeping, I got caught up. You seemed just so... happy." She smiled, thinking of Ace because he made her feel that way —happy.

"Me?" Shona replied then chuckled. "Well, that's a word no one has ever used to describe me, but okay."

She really wasn't. After that act X had put on in front of everyone, she went from happy to confused. She didn't know what she wanted anymore and with Chico reaching out to see if she had heard from him, she was about over it.

She knew he still cared, but she wondered was he even sure he was prepared for her to actually be with someone. She felt stupid too, especially since he could have easily gotten her number through his sister from Kaleela. So she had no desire to hear from him now.

Truthfully, the music was just her way of hyping herself up to get through the day without going off on Kaleela who was already pushing her buttons.

"No, I wasn't trying to offend you—" Gabby started before Shona stopped her.

"Girl, calm down," she said, laughing as she motioned for her to bring it down a notch with one hand. "Come, have a seat. You're tripping for real. And you're about to make me wonder who sent your ass."

Gabby looked around as if Shona was speaking to someone else. "Wait. Sent who? You mean me?"

"Yeah, you with your thick ass," she heard Kaleela say under her breath while Chaney was at the washbowl staring the entire time. She sucked her teeth, doing her best to ignore Kaleela. Their own on again/off again situation was off now, so they both were in a funk. She peeped Gabby too, admiring how well put together she was. Especially for a thick girl.

"Hush up, girl," Shona told her. Gabby was taken aback. Just a second ago, the same girl was about to kill her, but the look she had in her eyes now told Gabby she wanted something else.

Shona noticed Gabby's nails, inching closer to her to take a look. The funny thing was that they all were designed differently from acrylic to gel nails. Shona smiled thinking how genius it was to come in and basically show your work on your own nails. She still looked at her as being a tad bit off, but she did respect her for putting herself all out there.

It was as if Gabby had thought of everything a nail technician should know how to do from glitter, to spray, long to short. It looked crazy as hell having ten nails designed differently, but they were fierce at the same time.

"Damnnn," Shona whispered to herself, carefully examining them from the outside to underneath once she grabbed one hand at a time. "Oh yes, bitch. I see you," she said to no one in particular, causing Gabby to blush. She'd spent hours coming up with different ways to impress Shona and from the looks of it, she had.

"So," Shona spoke, finally releasing her fingers. "I must say you did your thing, girl. You're weird as hell like you missed your morning meds, but I'm used to it," he said, looking Kaleela's way. "And you most definitely can do some nails."

"Yes!" Gabby celebrated, then stopped, and covered her mouth with both hands. She didn't want to assume it was an automatic yes, but it certainly didn't sound like a no.

"Yo, you are too funny," Shona told her, shaking her head. "With your straight-laced self."

"Straight-laced?"

"Lame, green, naive', all that shit," Kaleela clarified for Gabby. "But I fucks with it."

"Well, okay," she agreed, shrugging her shoulders as she smiled all the while as Chaney fumed.

She accepted who she was long ago, but more time with Ace let her know there was more to her that even she hadn't discovered. They all seemed a bit rough, but nice. The place was definitely complete with high-end furniture and other accommodations which explained why The Palace was located on this side of town.

"So, how about this? You set your own prices, but I get three hundred dollars a week for the chair. But don't lowball yourself. You have skills." Gabby grinned, swaying when she said that part. "My weekday hours are seven in the morning to nine at night and eight in the morning to ten on Saturdays. We're closed on Sundays because even God rested."

"I'll take it!" Gabby said, lightly clapping her hands in excitement.

Shona laughed. "Lil' Gunna back there, who you've met, is my sister. She's Kaleela. She orders supplies, keeps the books, and is pretty much our own personal security. Now, don't let that wheelchair fool you. She's official, but I'm no slouch either. Your ass almost met Jesus a few minutes ago." Gabby did a little Holy Ghost shake, playing the role.

"No, don't do that again," Shona said with dipped brows until Gabby's smile dropped. "Girl, I'm kidding. Relax. You might as well get used to it."

"Oh, good," she giggled. She and women never really hung out, so she was going to have to figure this girlfriend thing out as she went.

"We have Remy, Shelby and Chaney, the other three beauticians. Then Marilyn who run the front. She isn't here now. She has school in the mornings two days a week. Take a walk around and then meet me in the back."

"Wow, this is rather impressive," Gabby admitted, taking a tour now of the entire salon, even the back areas where her office and supply room were.

"Shit, I'm impressed with you with your thick ass," Kaleela said, stopping right in front of her. She undressed Gabby with her eyes wondering if her decision to choose Chaney after breaking things off with Rainbow until Chaney cleared her throat. "I mean, keep walking. I'm taken. Abby."

That's the crap that kept her and Chaney at odds, but it was Chaney's fault. Until she put a stop to all of Kaleela's antics, they would always be at odds. Chaney was hoping with sobriety, they'd have monogamy, but Kaleela was proving that somethings just didn't change that easily or at all.

"It's Gabby."

"Same thang," Kaleela said, winking at Chaney.

"It's Gabby Wilcox. Well Gabriela, but I hate my real name, so just call me Gabby," she replied, looking at everyone who hadn't spoken but were definitely checking her out.

"Well, welcome to The Palace, Gabby. Kaleela's showed her ass already and as for the others, they will just talk about you later behind your back."

"Huh?" The other women snickered, while Chaney walked over and shook her hand, taking a look for herself.

"Hi, I'm Chaney. And I won't. I do my shit in your face unlike—."

"Ayyye," Remy said, cutting her off.

"See, I hadn't even said any names but the hit poodle hollered."

Shelby and Shona laughed at that, while Kaleela sat back watching Chaney and Gabby. If she could, she wanted them both in her bed at the same time. From what she could see, Gabby had the whole wide world in her pants. She wanted some of that.

"Well, nice to meet, Chaney. All of you," she said, waving at all the girls. "Thank you so very much," she then squealed, patting and rubbing Shona on the back who didn't seem to know what to do.

She mumbled a few words under her breath, praying she did the right thing. Nothing seemed normal in her life anymore, so she figured why not hired Gabby. She really did look harmless. She figured her bubbly, bright energy was needed around there anyway. Besides, she needed a nail technician and Gabby needed another reason to thank God she was still alive.

CHAPTER SEVENTEEN

After two months of working at The Palace, Ace found himself falling even harder. Gabby was not only working and earning her own money, but she was saving some to get her own shop one day. She refused any help, but he was secretly putting some money away for her.

They still hadn't done more than kiss or cuddle but she was looking beyond appetizing to him when he'd gotten off early on her off day. He noticed the additional weight she'd lost, a little upset about it, but he'd take her big or small. He'd cut Milky Way all the way off now, his boys teasing him.

He was backed up, often taking care of himself, but today he wanted more. He wanted *her*. He needed *her*. Gabriela was *her*.

"Hey," he said, catching her in the laundry room. She was in full wife mode, doing his laundry and pressing his clothes. He couldn't believe how a man could mistreat a woman let alone one as nurturing as her.

Her stretch pants and tank top melted against her skin, wearing a warm peach and gray color set. Her hair, pulled up high into a ponytail, exposed her neck. Like always, her scent excited him.

"Hey, Ace. You're home early," she said, turning around to greet him. He pulled her in, shrinking the space between them as he felt her warm skin against his.

"Yeah, I am," he said, holding her tighter as he gathered his thoughts. "I told you not to do my laundry, Gabriela, but thank you." He kissed the top of her head as she squeezed him. "You're acting like you missed me."

"I do," she told him softly, her cheek against his chest.

"Good, because we need to talk," he told her, reaching around his back to grab her hands. He felt her tense up, worry now in her eyes. "Naw, nothing like that."

"Oh, okay then. Let's talk," she said, following him into the kitchen. "Let me check the crockpot." He already knew it was chicken and dumplings. A dish his aunt taught her how to make in the crockpot. With working, she still made sure he had a home cooked meal, the crockpot being her friend.

"Gabriela, baby. Stop," he begged, sitting her on the kitchen counter.

"Whoaaa," she belted, laughing as she grabbed on to him. "You know it's unsanitary to sit me on the counter."

"Why? Because I would eat this pussy like it's dinner, Gabriela. Don't play," he said, a sly grin on his face.

He'd become more comfortable saying things to her like that, watching her eyes light up when he did. Still, they never crossed that line because she never gave him permission. That is, until she said something that shocked him, making his dick swell twice its size.

"Prove it," she whispered, biting her lip.

Unable to restrain himself any longer, he pulled her face to his, his mouth on top of hers. Before their lips fully connected, his tongue slowly glided in her mouth. It tasted sweet, just like candy. Ace felt his dick pressing hard against his pants as he explored her mouth, consuming the flavor.

Gabby, eager to taste him, welcomed the intrusion as her tongue tangled with his. Ace felt like a bitch, his dick in pain fighting to get out solely from a kiss. He'd been wanting to fuck her since they laid eyes on each other months ago. But once she'd gotten in his system and in his house, he was tired of fighting. He needed some pussy—her pussy.

"Uh," she moaned, as his mouth traveled to her jawline and down her neck. Wet kisses feeling like heaven were planted with such ease. To him she was so delicate, so gentle. If he fucked her right then, he felt he'd probably break her in half.

Feeling the hardness of her nipples through the tank top she wore wasn't helping at all. Sometimes he felt she purposely walked around in clothing that easily revealed the parts of her body he craved.

He tried to think of every excuse why he should stop, but none came. She was doing everything she needed to do to heal, so the guilt he once about wanting her had was now subsiding. He especially knew therapy was working, the nightmares almost gone as she slept quietly throughout most nights. And the nights she found herself in his bed, she wasn't whimpering like she used to. She just wanted to be held.

He quickly stopped, second-guessing himself. It had been six months, but after seven years with Tyson, he knew there was no way she was ready for him. He was bold, dominant, and even selfish, only letting Tyson live because he knew there was a part of her that still loved him.

"What?" she asked anxiously, trying to figure out why he stopped as she searched his eyes. She watched him close his and breathe before opening them again. He told himself that if she looked into his never breaking eye contact, he was going for it.

"Gabriela, baby. I'm a no-good ass dude. No shit, I really am. I ain't never loved a woman or even tried to. And you're fucking perfect." He stopped and swallowed hard, before he started again. "I have fucked multiple women, a lot of them." Gabby gasped, pulling away just a little.

"Girl, don't fucking play with me. All with protection. Hell, sometimes I fuck them right before I get here just to make sure I don't fuck you. But tonight, the only thing I can think about is making love to you."

"Oh." She wasn't so sure she was ready for such honesty, but she couldn't judge him for that. Not when he was telling her what she wanted to hear, what she needed to hear. That was him wanting her too.

She smiled, leaning his way again slowly where her arms wrapped themselves around his neck with ease. It felt safe. She liked that.

"So, you fucked them but you wanted to make love to me?" she asked, biting the bottom corner of her lip, realizing what he said and what that meant.

He shook his head yes, a sheepish grin appearing on his face. "But you got to teach me, teach me how to make love to you," he admitted, rubbing and admiring her thick ass thighs. "Shit," he mumbled to which she snickered. "I can give you a good fuck, but making love is something I've never done."

She pushed him back just enough to get down off the counter. "Well, let the lesson begin."

"Wait—" he said, trying to halt her. By then, she had slid down, squatting in front of him. His thick dick, fighting to be released, eagerly greeted her when she unzipped his jeans, freeing it as she went for it.

"Mmmmm," she moaned, taking him in her mouth. "So fucking good," she said.

Ace wanted to cry, hoping his dick didn't betray him while she hungrily slurped his girth and length like a champ. He couldn't believe her quirky ass came with a mouth that could do the shit she had just done.

"Please," he begged and laughed, hoping she didn't stop as she slowed down then held all of his dick in her hand.

"It's okay. Let me take care of you the way you've taken care of me." Before he could protest, she took him in again, dropping a glob of spit that now helped her stroke his shaft with ease.

"Fuck, Gabriela," he growled, running his fingers through her hair. "I'm fuck you real good, baby. Shit!" She giggled, winking her eye as she looked up at him with his dick still in her mouth. He roughly pushed her head down and she took all that dick in, making him stand on his tippy toes.

"Aww, fuck," he groaned, working her pretty ass mouth around his dick. It was wet, warm and where he wanted to be forever if he could. With head this good, he knew her pussy had to be better.

Then she stopped, snatching her head back.

"What—what's wrong, baby?" he quickly asked, ready to bust any second now.

"I thought we weren't fucking," she said lowly, poking her bottom lip out.

He laughed and bent down to kiss her, then said, "I got to fuck you once just to get that shit out my system. Then I'ma make love to you. Is that okay?"

"Un huh," she agreed. "I was just kidding. You taste so good. Oh, and the way you worked my mouth. Let me let me finish, Ace. I'm the teacher now."

"Who the fuck are you, woman?" he asked, ready to gobble her ass up.

"Whoever you want me to be." She was so fucking cute, her mouth wet from him being inside of it.

By the end of the night, Ace's mind was blown. They'd not only blessed the kitchen but almost every room of the house. He was lying on his back, with her on his chest. Both of their eyes were closed, but he was very much awake.

"I love you," he whispered. "Forever."

"You promise?" she replied, catching him off guard. He was sure she was knocked out. The house was dark and quiet short of her breathing, but he was wrong

"Fuck yeah," he said with such serious, she felt her body shiver as he looked down at her. "Even if he has to die, Gabriela. This right here has to be forever."

Ace Alexander shook his own head and laughed. He would have never thought he'd be locked down by one woman, but that was proof that in life, it just took the right woman to get the job done.

And Gabriela Wilcox was that bitch for the job.

CHAPTER EIGHTEEN

Since the day Kaleela came home, there wasn't a day that hadn't gone by, she didn't mention her friend Reagan. This was very different for her. This truly was the first time her closeness to a woman had nothing to do with sex. She had finally made found a real friend.

To her, they were stronger together, both fighting to stay sober. She could easily go back to the people and places she knew that embraced her, but to stay sober meant she had to make better choices.

Besides, going to club came with benefits like a free bottle of liquor and pussy. Over the years, both led to nothing but trouble.

"Kaleela, you ordered more towels?" Shona asked her, seeing the quality of the ones they had left use after use. Kaleela, responsible for inventory, came in a few times a week whenever she wasn't at a meeting. "Yea, Shona. Damn, how many times you gone ask me that?"

Kaleela was in a bad mood and had been since the day before. She messed around and went on Rainbow's page, watching all the traffic she was getting. Yes, she had cut her off to get right, but Rainbow hadn't tried one time to reach out.

No one knew the story behind the two of them but her. They'd met years ago before they linked up with Chico. Shona had been out all day, trying to steal food and a few outfits out of the store. Kaleela was tired of just hanging around not contributing. So, she went into the back of a grocery store where they threw out pastries and bread daily.

She heard someone screaming. The sound was muffled, but she was walking around until she saw two people behind a dumpster. Snatching out her switchblade, Kaleela slowly slid around taking a peek to see what they were fighting about.

She saw Rainbow, bleeding between her legs begging the man to stop. He stood up and kicked her between the legs and yelled, "So you give these lil' ass boys pussy, but not ya daddy? You slut, I take care of you and your crackhead mama. Got me out here all night and day looking for you and you sleep up under some cardboard boxes. Yeah, he told me where you were. See how these little boys will flip on you for a few dollars?" After delivering another kick, this time to her stomach, Kaleela jumped out and jumped on his back, stabbing him over and over.

"Arrgggh!" he screamed, blood spurring from his mouth and back. Kaleela swung one last time, hitting him in the side of his neck and he collapsed, still reaching out for her until he hit the ground.

"Runnnnn!" she screamed at Rainbow, as she laid there in shock. "Get out of here!" Rainbow, scrambling to pull her shorts up, finally took off leaving them there.

Kaleela found a book of matches, covered him up with nearby debris, and set him on fire, freeing Rainbow. She never knew while she'd set her free, she stop ed herself from moving forward.

After that day, she never saw her again until three years after she and Shona left the game. Kaleela, still in denial about being paralyzed, lived in the strip club. It felt familiar. She was still powerful and her name still had clout. Then one night, she damn near choked on a bottle of Patron when Rainbow walked out, her pussy lips waving at her.

She pushed this stripper, Candy Girl, off her lap, making her way to the stage. Kaleela felt a high she hadn't felt since the night they met, that pulled her in. She was high off the memory of Rainbow, often wondering whatever happened to her.

She motioned her over with her finger, and Rainbow not missing a beat stepped down off the stage and straddled her. Kaleela went in, tonguing her down and slipping two fingers in her pussy. Rainbow's back arched and she rode them motherfuckers out, coming two times on her hand.

When the song was over, Kaleela whispered in her ear, telling her to meet her outside in fifteen minutes. Instead of saying no, Rainbow practically wobbled off the stage. In not time at all, she was sitting on her face in the back seat of her truck.

She'd been stuck, sucking on her pussy ever since. The only problem was Rainbow would come and go, sometimes for months at a time. Kaleela, not trusting what they had, then turned to other women resuming all of her hoe tendency antics. It was women like Chaney that got caught up in that web, often getting pieces of Kaleela. Pieces that usually didn't amount to much outside of the bedroom.

"So, you still acting like I'm not here?" she heard Chaney say, coming into the back office and closing the door. "Dang, Kaleela. It's been what now, two months?"

Kaleela looked up at her, then back down going through the receipts. To her, Chaney was cool. She fucked with her, but she'd warned her to not catch feelings and that's exactly what she had done.

In some ways, it wasn't even about her not wanting to be with Chaney. It was about Rainbow somehow always needing her, and her feeling the need to save her like she did before. It made her feel powerful, larger than life and it didn't hurt Rainbow was a big ass freak. She'd do all kinds of things to Kaleela most women wouldn't, so she held a spot for her that no one else seemed to fill..

Chaney, however, was built differently, stepping out there and making a name for herself. She had her own money, cars, clothing and even the finest jewelry, but she remained humble still living off 62nd Street and 12th in the Pork and Beans project. She was born there and she was okay with dying there. Kaleela knew that was a choice, not knocking Chaney, but she felt like your money should make you want to move around.

"Lock the door," she told Chaney, chewing the inside of her jaw. She was debating if she was going to fuck her right there or not since they were so called "off" right now.

Chaney was making it hard, wearing a pair of skinny jeans that snugly hugged her hips just below her navel, showing her belly piercing and vine-like tattoo that wrapped itself around her waist. Her top spared nothing, showing her breasts that were naturally round and firm in a short reggae color top with some high-top, reggae color Chucks.

Chaney had a style of her own, never comparing herself to anyone. But when it came to Kaleela, she cared more than she wanted to. Kaleela was a pretty stud known to have even prettier bitches on her arm, so to her, she had to turn heads. Especially Kaleela's.

"Okay," she said too quickly, turning the lock. She turned around and smiled, feeling nervous now that she had all of her attention.

"Tell me why you want me to fuck you so bad," she asked Chaney, peeping how eager she was to be in all in her personal space. Kaleela continued to work, staring a her from her periphery view until she slid her paperwork to the side, facing her.

"Kaleela, are you serious?" she asked, dropping her mouth.

"Pfft, hell yeah. Girl, you're celebrity status when it comes to clientele. I be on all yo' lil' pages with your friendly ass. You got rappers and video vixens shouting you out, showing you love. So don't lie. Now, tell me why you want to fuck with? So you can tell my people like this is some kind of competition?"

"In competition with who, Kaleela?" she asked looking around, snaking her neck. Chaney hadn't seen Rainbow with her in months. As far as she knew, they were done. Either way, she wasn't checking for Rainbow because her heart wanted Kaleela.

"Girl, gone. When I first hit that, you knew about Rainbow. You even told me you were down for a threesome, but it was my bitch that said no. Wait," she said, holding her hand up with her head tilted to the side. "Or maybe you think I'm your charity case. Is that it?" she asked, her lips pursed. "Yeah, let me go holla at Kaleela's drunk ass before she kill herself. You know she already can't walk."

Chaney stood there in shock with her mouth wide open. Her feelings were hurt, but most importantly, she was hot.

"Yeah, I said it. I'm tired of people hurting me. That's why I fuck you hoes and move the fuck on. Why? So I can show y'all I still got the juice." Kaleela smiled, dragging her tongue across the top of her teeth.

"That couldn't be further from the truth," Chaney replied, through clenched teeth. "But guess what? I don't even care anymore. You got your tongue stuck so far up a traitorous hoe's pussy, you can't see a solid bitch when she shows up for you.

You, a charity case? Kaleela, back in the day bitches and even dude's dicks who knew you were gay, still got hard whenever you pulled up on the scene. They had bets about who was gone put some dick in you. Your ass had the best of both worlds and you know it too."

Chaney was infuriated, fighting hard not to cry. Kaleela felt a knot in her stomach, but instead of acknowledging it, she chuckled, dismissing what she heard.

Chaney shook her head, knowing this was a lost cause. Everything about Kaleela was always about Kaleela. No one else mattered. Well, no one else but Rainbow. Chaney knew plenty about Rainbow, but chose not to shit on her name. If she was going to be Kaleela's girl, it had to happen because they both wanted it. Not because she played dirty or brought about bitch down to get her.

"Niggas thought that about me?" Kaleea asked proudly more so to herself, rubbing her chin.

"See? Still stuck on how hard people wanted you," Chaney scoffed, looking at her in disbelief. "Kaleela, I would see you and sit outside all day just to hear you laugh and talk shit to people. Some days, just seeing you ride by and jump out and smoke with your crew was enough to make my day.

I would even get up on my tippy toes just to see you slam the dice down in a dice game, niggas all hovering around you. So hell yeah, I woulda fucked your girl just as long as I got a piece of you. *You are Kaleela!*" she yelled, clapping her hands to make a point.

And back then, I wasn't shit for you to look at. I know I was dirty, wearing the same clothes over and over. My momma wasn't shit and my grandma didn't know how to say no, giving her money every time she showed up. But you know what? Thank you," she said, walking to the door and unlocking the lock as she prepared to leave.

I appreciate you showing me just how clueless and far gone *you* truly are. Just remember this when that hoe shows you why they call her Rainbow. The bitch fruity and got more faces than a band of dollar bills. And when I walk out this door, cancel my subscription to your fucked up world. I'm good on you." She snatched open the door, slamming it on her way out.

Kaleela jumped, feeling some type of way. She knew Chaney had feelings, but this was deeper than sex. She wasn't expecting all of that, but something made her feel like she was making another mistake. She knew Rainbow wasn't shit, but she felt she wasn't either. Feeling the urge to drink to numb all of her emotions, she snatched her cell out of her pocket and called up Reagan.

"Hey, Ka leee leeee," she sang.

"Hoe, don't be calling me that," Kaleela laughed, masking her frustration. "You'on want me calling you Rey Rey."

"That's because someone already calls me Rey Rey," she replied, referring to Gator.

Even though he was keeping his distance, Regan still had hope. What she didn't know was that Gator secretly kept up with her through X to see if she was dating and staying sober. Even though he loved her, he knew an addict. They would lie and do it easily to the ones they loved.

If he knew about her abortion, he'd be devastated. So Reagan made sure that never slipped out her mouth to anyone. Not even to Kaleela. She was ashamed, but scared her child would have been born damaged due to her reckless ways.

So she through herself into work, transitioning back into the real world by earning a paycheck. This time, instead of working from home, she and her AA mentor agreed she needed to be around people in a stimulating environment. She had learned that one of her triggers was isolation, so going to and from work with X each day proved to be healthy as she remained sober.

It also helped he stayed sniffing any cup she had. She wanted to get mad, but decided it was because he loved her. At least someone did since she was pretty sure Gator didn't.

From the looks of it, many would agree. He fell into a routine, hitting up clubs with Tooley, sometimes with X. He was even dating and fucking, although meaningless fucks. Still none compared to Reagan. So he stopped trying to replace her and just live until love seemed possible again while Reagan prayed each day he'd let her back in.

"Girl, you're like me," Kaleela told her "We are dating two damn ghosts," she said, speaking on Rainbow and Gator."

"Says who?" Reagan quickly asked, her face balled up.

"Says karma. The bitch finally came for us," she admitted, frustrated that she was thinking about Chaney after the way she treated her.

"Well karma better sit her ass down because Gator is mine," Reagan said with authority. "I'm just giving him time to get his mind right. I let his ass play, but you best believe the minute I call, he's coming," she bragged, but truthfully, even she didn't believe that. She just figured if she said it enough, it would come true.

"Oh, hold on. I see X walking in," she told her before she called out to him. "X, what time are we leaving today?"

Kaleela felt like Reagan and X were another version of her and Shona. She even tried to get all four of them to link up, but Shona was being standoffish. She used to probe, asking Kaleela when's the last time she saw him. Now she acted like she hated his guts if his name came up.

"Girl, you heard that?"

"What?" Kaleela was hoping it was something she could tell Shona to get her mad. She was over her sister pretending to be okay when she really did want company that was a female and related to her.

""Ugh, I wish you would! I will tell Mama on you!" Reagan said instead to him, not answering Kaleela. "You know she don't play about me!" she told him, rolling her eyes.

"Shorty, you're worse than me. I bet you rolling your eyes," Kaleela said, laughing. "I thought I was spoiled, but damn."

"Naw, he's taking his little frustrations out on me. Ever since his psychotic ex started up again with her nonsense, he's in a bad mood."

Hearing him say ex, Kaleela perked up a bit.

"Ex?"

"This bitch Avery, the absolute worst. I told you about that whore. She came home with a fucking condom inside of her. Who does that? Just eww," Reagan said lowly, hoping X didn't hear her. She wanted to beat Avery's ass, but she knew she'd violate probation, so Avery got a pass.

"Yeah, I would have to kill that hoe for real," Kaleela said, rather glad her sister's temporary interest in him had waned. She'd die for Shona before she allowed her to be in the streets dealing with the likes of his ex who couldn't let go.

"Exactly. But X will save the hoe at a distance talking about ignore her. That's X trying to control me, but it's whatever. I got something for that bitch, " she fussed, packing up her stuff. "Then I'm out of there. It's my own place if not with Gator."

Reagan watched X fussing on his cell. He walked back and forth inside his office. He was so mad, she could see the veins forming a line across his temples.

"Girl, he is cursing somebody out. Probably that thirsty trick carrying on. Her ass more than likely need a fix and any old dick just won't do," Reagan said, giggling.

"I like them feisty," Kaleela said, wagging her tongue. "If I snatch her ass up for him, do I get to fuck?" she asked.

"Ugh, is that all you think about?" Reagan asked, watching him come her way fuming. "Never mind," she whispered, covering her mouth. "Remember, I'm coming through there. What time you get home?"

"Umm," Kaleela said, looking at her watch. "In about an hour."

"Get some snacks. I'ma tell him to drop me off to a friend. What Shona got planned tonight?"

"Not shit, aggravating me like she the police. It don't matter though, come through. Your brother's gone get it."

Kaleela didn't want to be alone. She never did, and she was doing her best to stay away Rainbow. Especially since Chaney wasn't fucking with her because of her ex. Still, she needed some pussy, so Chaney better act right sooner than later.

"Or your sister is," Reagan shot back. "They both are playing. Anyway, text me some stuff you want me to bring and hurry up," she whispered, giving him her back as he walked up.

"He knows where we stay?" she asked, all confused now looking at

Chaney's Twitter account. She touched the screen across her face, biting her bottom lip.

"I don't know," she replied lowly, letting her know he was in listening distance. X frowned at her, shaking her head.

"Just guide him in. I can't wait," Kaleela laughed. She wasn't sure how Shona would respond, but they both needed to get their shit together. Her with Chaney and Shona with anybody, but it might as well be X.

He wasn't the type Kaleela felt met the profile for Shona who was still hood in her own prissy way, but one thing she knew. He'd definitely had Shona in her feelings. They were about to see where this went, praying it didn't backfire on them.

"Me either," she said, smiling at X as he appeared in her face.

"What the hell you're smiling for?" he asked her, squinted his eyes. He knew Reagan. She was sneaky as fuck.

"Why are you all in my business?"

"I wouldn't if you drove your own damn car."

"Well, I didn't," she shot back. She then whispered to Kaleela, "I gotta go." Hanging up, Reagan smiled as they executed their plan.

They hung up, both feeling hyped about their plans. Coming out from the back, Chaney remained true to her word. She didn't even bat an eye at Kaleela, ignoring her as she talked and walked all by her.

Kaleela wanted to knock her fine ass her down, mad she was committing to this act like they were nothing. They were beyond nothing, Kaleela remembering the last time she had Chaney's ass all in her mouth. The passion marks she'd left on her ass cheeks made her own center jump thinking about it.

To avoid fucking Chaney up who was wearing the hell out of a black and gold puma top and tights with gold Pumas, she slid to the front where Marilyn were laughing and watching YouTube. No one cared that she and Chaney were on a real time out and that was fucking with her.

Remy, on the phone like always, definitely didn't even though she stayed getting the latest tea like now. If anyone needed to know who shot who on any given day in the hood or who got who pregnant, hit up Remy. She was a walking social media post.

"Hey, sis. When's the last time you spoke to X?"

"Who?" she asked her, looking all confused. Shona knew exactly who X was but she wasn't sure why Kaleela was asking.

"Come on, now. You know Reagan's brother, X."

"That tall, light-skinned dude with the pretty teeth and lips that be dropping her off up here sometimes?" Marilyn asked, getting all excited. Shona had no clue X had even been up there, cutting her eyes at Shona.

"What?" she faked confused.

"Nothing, bitch," Shona grumbled, putting her earpods in her ear as she whipped out the pack of hair she needed to die for her early morning appointment the next day.

"Yeah, him, but don't play, hoe. That's my sis man all day."

"He is?" Remy asked in disbelief, snatching her cell away from her ear.

"Oh oh," Shelby said under her breath, laughing. She was finishing up one of the flyest cuts. If Shelby couldn't do anything in life, she could cut some hair. "Watch her timeline in 5, 4, 3, 2—"

Remy sucked her teeth, before attending to her call. They could hear some girl yelling all in the background. Remy jumped right in where she left off, realizing there was no gossip to give or listen to.

"Well, he's not. He's arrogant, rude as fuck and most definitely not my type. Besides, I am not looking for a relationship. Now, dick he can give me, but keep all of that emotional stuff away from me."

Kaleela smirked and waved her hand at her. "Girl, that's not even you. Since when you have had sex for fun?"

"But it's definitely you," she heard Chaney mumble, while pulling the needle and thread through as she did her fifth client's head for that day.

Kaleela struggled not to lash out, since she deserved that, but Chaney was pushing it. Most bitches only got to came at her once disrespectfully before she reminded them who the fuck she was. Chaney got a pass, but Kaleela was adding those passes up in her head. She promised herself the moment Chaney gave in, she was going to murder the pussy.

All the girls laughed at Chaney and Kaleela, wondering when that emotional tussle would get physical. Especially Remy. She kept her cell ready to go live.

"Well, X was dropping Reagan off tonight, but I told her it's best she get someone else," she lied, trying to gauge Shona's reaction.

"I don't care," she lied, rolling her neck around, a tell tale sign when she did. It was like pushing out a lie would get stuck in her throat, making Kaleela chuckle. "They are your company if they do. Just keep it down because I'm calling it an early night," she said, hoping Kaleela really didn't have him coming by there.

"He's not. Meeting's cancelled tonight and Reagan just wanted to chill."

"Okay, Kaleela," she said, giving her her back. She was just glad she hadn't relapsed. That meant if her house was the meeting spot for a night, it was better than bailing her out of jail or worse, identifying her in a morgue.

"Oh, I might have a friend come through for me, too. I ain't got no ole lady, so," she said, staring hard at Chaney who was starting to tear up. "I'll just grab some wings. Feed her and shit before she feed me."

Chaney's cell rang. When she picked up, she wiped her tears and smiled. In fact, the entire time she was on the phone, she was smiling. Kaleela didn't like that shit one bit, eager to snatch her cell away.

"Bitches be frontin'," she said loud enough to get Chaney's attention. She told the person hold on, walking outside to finish her call. Kaleela sucked her teeth as she walked by, wishing she didn't care so much now. "Shona why y'all women be lying so much? Talking about you just want the dick."

"I do," she said, tapping her last client on the shoulder who had fallen asleep. She was glad when her dryer stopped, ready to go home. Just that quickly, Kaleela had her in a bad mood. "Just haven't had time to find one to fall on top of."

"Girl," she drawled, rolling her eyes at her sister. See what I mean, Shelby?"

"Un huh," was all Shelby said.

She stayed in her lane. Shona was her boss while Kaleela would fuck her up for disagreeing if she was really mad. Unlike Remy and Chaney, she knew what Kaleela was capable of when her head wasn't in a good space. She'd been watching her and Chaney for weeks, wondering when that would come to a head. And the longer Chaney stayed outside, she saw it happening really soon.

"You're right. I'm good on men and X is a little too pretty for me. I like them rough. Real rough, slapping me around and all," she said, grinning as she stuck her tongue out.

Shona was lying, goose bumps forming even then as she pictured him, how good he looked both times she saw him. He was cocky and a know it all, but with the way she was feeling right now, he could bust it wide open in front of everyone and she wouldn't think twice about it. She'd been fucking him in her dreams since that night, almost snatching the rollers out of her client's head.

"A'ight, enough of that," Kaleela told her as Chaney continued to talk off in the cut. "Let's go. I told you I have this bitch that's been hitting my line. She might fall through and you playing, sis."

Chaney then walked by smoothly, passing her as she said nothing. She picked up the needle and thread, finishing up her client's sew-in. That knot Kaleela used to feel in her stomach for Rainbow formed, making her angry with herself.

"Not tonight, Kaleela. You've been doing good. Meetings and all," Shona said, blowing her cover. She had blocked almost her entire contact list. Her next step was deleting them. She was hoping Chaney would give her reason to do that.

"True," Kaleela said, wanting to say more. "Well, the meetings help. Keeps me accountable so I can be accountable to other shit in my life," she said, looking Chaney's way. "I made some fucked up choices and I'm still paying for them. I might need some help with that, though. What do you think?"

"What kind of help?" she asked, looking confused.

"I don't know, maybe helping me make amends with a few people. You know I'm not good with that shit at all," she said, her eyes dropping as she grabbed the bridge of her nose.

Shona finished with the client she was working on, adding a few bobby pins in there so it would stay secured. As her client went to pay, Shona stared at her sister for the first time today and saw something that scared her—fear.

"Well, we're Bradley's," she said, walking up to her and kneeling down. "There is nothing we can't do. Let's talk about it later, okay. I got you."

"You got me?" she asked, looking at her sister and smiling.

"Hell yeah, I got you, silly girl. Now help me clean up so we can get out of here. Even if my evening is going to be the usual, I'm glad you're having Reagan come over. I may not fuck with her brother, but she seems like she's pretty cool people."

"And she's just a friend," Kaleela threw in there quickly.

Shona laughed. "I know that."

Chaney stopped what she was doing as they talked, looking over her shoulders. Whens he did, their eyes met and instead of Kaleela being her usual self saying something slick, she saw sorrow in her eyes. For once, she felt maybe they both were tripping.

She smiled at her, dropping her head before she went back to work on her client's head. She wasn't so sure, but she could have sworn she saw Kaleela's face relax, a faint smile forming.

Shelby had already left by then and Marilyn was waiting until the bus came for her six o'clock class up the street at the university.

"Chaney, y'all good?" Shona asked her, while Remy kept talking on the phone.

"I think we're good," she said, looking at Kaleela once more. Kaleela couldn't help herself. She was about to go crazy if she didn't say something before she left out of there. Rolling over, she shot her shot and asked, "You sure *you're* good?"

"Not really, but I can't chase what don't want to be caught, right?" She looked at Kaleela, feeling a tightness in her chest. Shona was putting the towels used for the day in the washer, giving them a brief moment to themselves. A tear threatened to fall, but Chaney caught it before it did.

"No one ever wanted you to chase, girl. Things just got...I don't know, weird."

"Weird?" Chaney said, shaking her head. "Hey, I guess my love is weird then. Cool. Let me take this call," she said, scurrying off before Kaleela could stop her.

"Damn, she getting a lot of calls," she said to herself, not like it one bit. But the problem wasn't Chaney, it was her. She knew it too. It always had been.

While Chaney escaped to whatever had her excited, even if it could be a façade, Kaleela took off, remembering she'd left something in her office. She'd been holding out on it for a while, wondering if now was a good time to bring it out. When she got there, she quickly locked her door, anxious to get to it.

"Yes," she cheered silently, pulling out a water bottle. She stared at it, licking her lips, the more she stared, however, the more anxious she'd become. Probably because it wasn't water.

It was tequila.

She knew if she let it touch her lips, there was no turning back. At least not right away. She stopped and looked up, feeling like someone staring at her, when she heard a tapping on the door.

"Night!" Shona yelled as a sign she was heading home. "Kaleela, hurry up!"

"Kaleela? Kaleela, are you in there?" Chaney asked.

Slowly untwisting the lid, Kaleela sniffed it and sighed. She tossed it in the trashed before she opened the door. The look on Chaney's face told it all. She was going down a slippery slope and fast, starting with the woman standing before her if she let her walk. That pressure was getting real, too real, wishing she had something strong to kill that pounding in her chest.

CHAPTER NINETEEN

Reagan had not only talked X into dropping her off once he realized where they were going, but she'd even got him to help her carry the groceries to the front door. He had already had a stressful day, dealing with his ex and then a strange package delivered to his office with no return addressed, making his head pound all the more.

These headaches had been something he was damn near married to most of his life as a kid. He often attributed his dark mood and temper to them, brooding as they always seemed to hover around, but today was one of the worst ones. Still, he dealt with Reagan as much as he could with no attitude since it really wasn't her fault until she pushed his buttons.

He decided getting her out of his car and fast was the best way to get rid of trigger number—his annoying, baby sister. During the ride, he gritted his teeth hearing Regan chatter after a tedious shopping spree in the grocery store making them fight through five o'clock traffic. Although he was ready to pull off, X knew he couldn't leave her to struggle with the bags as she now pouted when he initially refused to move.

He also needed to talk to Ace and fast about that package. Being an attorney came with creating a long line of enemies, but being as bold to send something to his office didn't sit too well with him. They were asking to be dealt with and he was ready. Just not the legal way. So instead of reporting it, he left it unopened, tossing it in his truck.

"Let me help this girl," he huffed under his breath, turning his car off. Besides, he was also curious as to what their house looked like on the inside. He heard Kaleela stayed over here, but he wasn't sure if she stayed with her sister or not. Like Shona, X was too fucked up to hit Shona up, but too intrigued to forget her. And from what he could tell, they both had fucked up attitudes that needed work.

Not wanting to create any drama that could disturbed Reagan's sobriety and new friendship with Kaleela, he stayed away after their little exchange but it didn't mean he was happy about it.

When they pulled up, he didn't see the truck she drove that night, making his eagerness turn to anxious. Still curious to see if she was there, he hit the locks to get out. Even this kick ass headache he was having couldn't stop him now.

As they got closer to the front door, he remembered how alluring she was that day. A natural beauty at that beyond the weave and lashes he knew probably came with her being a beautician and salon owner. Even underneath all of that, Shona's rawness was contagious, making him pick up his step just to get to her or so he hoped.

She had an edge to her that spoke boss bitch, but her wardrobe told him she did like the finer things in life. A perfect package, concluding he was indeed into Shonasia Bradley. He just had a lot of shit in his life and the main one was Avery. So today was just a day to quench his thirst and send him back to his complicated, cold-hearted lifestyle if he were so lucky to see her.

"You better be glad me and my boys cancelled pool tonight, Reagan," he told her, pretending to be mad. He was carrying two bags of two-liter sodas, ice and cups.

Reagan turned around and asked, "So that means Gator is free tonight? And if he is, who is he spending it with?"

"Do I look like I keep tabs on that man, girl? Hell if I know. Last I checked, he's grown and *single*," he said with an attitude, the sun beating down on his back. "Knock on the door."

Reagan rolled her eyes, knocking on the door with a matched attitude. "He ain't single, X. We are just on a break."

"No, *you're* on a break. My boy is free. Very free at that," he said, smiling as he remembered the last time he was at the strip club. This time instead of Ace going to the private room, Gator went and was back there most of the night.

He didn't trip, knowing how his sister played one of his closest friends. As long as he didn't while they were together, what Gator did was Gator's business. He just wanted his sister to focus on staying clean.

"I got something for that," she mumbled, calling his cell. After it rang and went straight to voicemail, she tried again only to get the voicemail again. X watched her catching a mini temper tantrum, cracking him up.

"That's funny, huh?" she said, hoping Shona shut him down.

"Knock on the door again," he told her, ready to get rid of these bags once he, realized they were still outside.

He couldn't lie, he felt butterflies in his stomach but would never admit that shit to anyone. To that, he reached past her, placing the bags down before he gave the door five, firm knocks.

Knock, knock, knock, knock, knock!

"Kaleela! Tell your friends we have a doorbell," Shona shouted from the inside before heading to the door. She swung it open hard and wide. As soon as she saw him, she was so taken aback that she forgot to breathe.

"Ah, hey Shona," Reagan said with a nervous laugh, uncertain what to do now that their plan began to unfold. "Everything's okay?"

X's attitude quickly dissipated, feeling that giddy shit as he stared at the view. Shona had just taken a shower, walking around in her nightshirt that hung just below her butt cheeks. She mostly stayed in her room when Kaleela had company and today would be no different. Now, she couldn't remember why she was even mad.

"Move, sis," he said, slowly walking up on her. He was beyond happy to see her. X's eyes traveled up and down her body, only finding perfection.

He had to move slowly or risk getting cursed and put out. Shona, unlike the other woman he randomly dealt with, was a different breed. She was that chick, a boss and a beauty that could have him by his balls. He knew it and that scared him. Still, in true X fashion, he had to be the asshole.

Shona, staring at him in awe, soon remember why he was so unforgettable, his finely line goatee thinly wrapped around his lip as he smiled. She appreciated a beautiful set of white teeth, too. She tried not to look, but she couldn't help it.

Reagan, waiting for her to move, giggled as Shona became immobilized in his presence. X had her and all he did was show up. To her, he was just her big head old brother, but she could tell he'd put a spell on Shona and from the looks of it, she'd put one on him too.

X carefully stroked her cheek, saying nothing and everything at the same time. Two strangers who knew nothing about each other, but enough to know they both were damaged were stuck, neither ready to move.

Proof Shona was as she unconsciously leaned into his touch, enjoying the roughness of his hand. He leaned in closer and whispered, "If this is what I would get everyday when I come home to you, then fuck it, I'm home."

"Please," she said, taking a step back once she realized what had happened. She shamefully had gotten lost, studying his wet lips that curled slight with one swipe of his tongue. "This is not *your* home, sir."

X laughed. "You're right, but it doesn't mean it can't be," he said, stepping closer towards her.

Reagan, with her lips turned up. This was getting to be too much, picking up the bags he left on the ground herself.

"Boy, leave this woman alone," Reagan finally said, pushing him to the side. She quickly gave Shona a short but warm hug before going inside.

"Kaleela!" Reagan yelled down the hallway where their bedrooms were. "Where do you want me to put this stuff? On the counter or refrigerator?"

Shona gasped when he decided to push it, gently cupping her right ass cheek. "Precious, the sooner you let me in, the sooner you'll see how much you want me to come home. Stop being so fucking mean," he whispered in her ear, causing her eyes to flutter.

"That's what I'm talking about! X, come through bro-in-law!" Hearing Kaleela's voice, Shona pushed him away and shot her sister a dirty look.

"You know you ain't loyal to no damn body," she hissed, putting her hand on her hip before she looked back at him. "Do you know what happened to the last man that touched me but wasn't ready to come home to me every day?"

X shrugged his shoulders and said, "No and I really don't give a fuck. That's why I'm here now. Gone on in so I can help put all that stuff away or whatever y'all doing with it."

"Them. Not me."

"Whatever," he said, easing past her as he winked before he following the girls in the kitchen.

"Excuse me. You are so rude," Shona grunted, her skin warm and red now.

"If she thinks that was rude, she might not be able to handle him," she heard Reagan mumble under her breath. X told her to shut up before he mushed her in the face. "Stop it, boy! Ugh!"

"I'm gone," Shona said under her breath to no one, watching his jawline twitch as he eyes landed her way. "Kaleela, have fun. Make sure the door is locked after *he* leaves. Thank you."

She didn't wait to get a response, taking off to her room and slamming the door.

Boom!

She exhaled, throwing her back against the door. She couldn't believe she'd let him in her head just that quickly. She could hear them all out there laughing, feeling like a fool. She grabbed a pillow, fell back on the bed and covered her face, grunting in frustration. Her mind was all over the place, but her body...her body was on fire. It needed to be touched. It needed him.

"I'm such a hoe," she said and laughing, tossing the pillow off her face. She then laid there basking in the sound of what could be family on the other side of the door. She liked that. She liked it a lot.

"I think she's big mad," Kaleela told X, popping a meatball in her mouth.

"You better stop doing that," Reagan warned her. "I think you like balls in your mouth."

"Yo, don't be saying that shit around me, girl. I don't want to hear that gay shit," he fussed, really mad about Shona pretending like he wasn't there. He'd been fooling himself all of this time, ready to go back there to check her. His life was already demanding. He didn't need a woman that would make it harder, his headache reminding him of that, too. Still, he needed to see her again.

"Reagan, he's pouting, girl. Guess he's mad, too. It's contagious!" Kaleela and Reagan got a kick out of his face all balled up, staring back and forth from them to Shona's door down the hall.

Kaleela couldn't remember a time where being sober so much fun. She was glad they'd both came by. She knew they pulled a dirty stunt on X and Shona, but something told her X was the cure for her sister's funk.

Reagan just wanted to distract him from all the drama that came with Avery, but she wouldn't have minded if X and Shona hooked up. He was the kind of man even she wanted, especially when she thought of their no good ass father.

X was smart, giving, although somewhat insensitive and mean, but he loved and protected those he loved with his life. By the time they stopped laughing, X was gone.

Still pouting on her bed, she laid with her legs crossed. She realized it wasn't even about sex anymore. It was him, consuming her thoughts and to know he was right outside of that door, frustrated the hell out of her until the door opened.

Fuck, she thought to herself, her mouth agape.

And like the cocky motherfucker he was, he eased on in with a smile on his face. He raised both hands in the air, ordering her to shut up without even speaking coupled with that look of a lifted right brow.

"That's your problem. You talk too much."

"I—"

"Shhhh," he demanded, rubbing his temples. "If I wanted all of that, I would have stayed out there with them."

She could tell he was in pain, her attitude subsiding just a little. "And?"

"And that's it, shit. I've been working almost twelve hour days for weeks, running her back and forth because her ass won't drive only to be tricked into coming here."

"Tricked?" she asked him with a disgusted look on her face. "Well, don't be tricked—leave."

"Look," X said, taking a minute to get his thoughts together.

He knew his headache wasn't her fault. It was the build up of bullshit, that package showing up either not helping. She was scowling now, her muscles tight as she sat up and clenched her fists.

"Chill," was all he said, looking around until he planted his ass on the edge of her bed near her. She was about to kick him when he spoke, rendering her speechless now.

"I did this tonight for Reagan because when it comes to her, I'll do almost anything. I had a fucked up day and honestly, the shit was getting worse until I saw you," he admitted, surprising himself.

He looked at her as some sort of place to play and forget about everything.

Besides, he wasn't exactly perfect himself. He had a dark past that he wanted to stay hidden, but Avery wasn't allowing him to do that. That's what she called and threw in his face earlier. He was about to break, needing a release and then this happened.

She happened.

Shona happened.

He was aggravated but when he saw her, he felt somewhat lighter, wanting to forget about his real life and live just a little inside of hers.

Shona felt something when he said that, sitting up on her elbows. That mean look she wore like a fulltime mask had somewhat softened, feeling the same way about Kaleela. In that moment, she knew they were more alike than not, no matter what side of town they grew up on or did for a living.

"I get it," she said, staring at the creased lines on his forehead. She could relate as she watched him roll his neck around, trying to relieve the pain.

"Precious, I ain't gone touch you. Just let me chill right here.

Reagan don't get out much anymore and something about your loud mouth sister makes her happy, so I'm happy," he told her, sitting on the edge of her bed.

"What do you call me that?"

"What, precious?" he laughed, shaking his head. He could see past that tough exterior, even more now as she said up close to him.

"Yes. Why?"

"Shit, cause you are. Any man can see you're more than just some tits and ass. And for the record, your body is banging as fuck, but your heart," he said, leaning over and bumping her shoulder. "That shit is good."

"How do you know that?" she asked lowly, her voice shaky.

"The night you came for your sister, how you supported her at graduation, too. Hell, how you've been taking care of her all of your life." She wondered how he knew those things, afraid to stare at him out of fear she'd just fall back and give him the pussy.

"Yes, she's tough with her slick mouth," he added, laughing. "You know I would love to kick her ass sometimes."

"And then you would have to deal with me," she shot back quickly, giving him a look.

X hollered then. "See what I mean? That," he said, pointing at her heart. "That right there deserves to be taken care of."

Shifting, Shona tucked her hair behind her ear. He was so close, talking like he knew her. He'd damn near undressed her mentally and emotionally, yet he hadn't even touched her.

"Well, I was just doing what anyone else would do that loves you." She went back to her cocoon, shrinking as he seemed to make himself more comfortable as he leaned against her body.

"Let me ask you this then," he said. When he did, he lightly stroked her milky thigh with one finger.

Goosebumps appeared but she didn't flinch, her eyes watching it travel up and down until he planted the palm of his hand across her thigh. It was warm, strangely soft but he was all man, feeling the strength in his hand when he gave her thigh a little squeeze. She gasped just a little, their eyes connecting when she did.

Then he asked, "Who's taking care of you?" She tucked her lips, looking away as she shrugged.

Shona crossed her arms, shaking her head as her kitty jumped. She wanted to tell him to take the pussy and never give it back to her, but she couldn't.

Her heart was too fragile for that and what little ego she had left was barely hanging on to a thread. Xander West had officially mind fucked her and had barely touched her.

She did no more about him then she would ever admit, taking peeks and glimpses of his life on social media. She knew how hard he went for people that didn't have such a perfect life and it was because of that, she was even more intrigued by him.

She got up, walking to the bathroom.

"Aye, where are you going?"

"Shhh," she told him, flipping his ego back on him.

When she came back out, she held a box of BC powder in her hand. It was for headaches. Kaleela used them like candy after a hang-over, so she kept a huge stash at the house. She had an unopened water bottle on her dresser, grabbing it and handing both to him. "Here. It tastes like shit, but take it. It will make you feel better."

He grabbed both, holding on to her hand and said, "I know what would make me feel better."

"Thank you for giving me my hand back," she said, prying her hand out of his. "Now take it and get some rest. No touching, either. I had a long day, too." She plopped down on the bed and propped her head up.

He knew what she was doing.

"So, this is the part where you prove you take care of others but stop them from taking care of you?" he asked as he stood.

"Maybe," she said with a shrug. He tossed the powdered aspirin in his mouth, chasing it down with the entire bottle of water. As he gulped it down, Shona felt her pussy throb almost uncontrollably. Oh how she wanted his lips and tongue to be all over her. He was so fucking sexy.

He looked down and smiled, wiping the water that dribbled down his chin. Shona tucked her lips in, but stared straight at the TV. It was on, but no sound. Something she did to go to sleep at night.

He slowly loosened his tie and unbuttoned his shirt. He watched her squirm, but she never asked him why he was taking his clothes off. Then his slacks came down right before his t-shirt came over his head.

Standing there like he owned her space, Shona wanted to thank all of the angels in heaven for dropping him in her life on today. He smiled, loving how cute she looked, her chinky eyes struggling not to look at him.

She watched him slide his hand down his stomach until it slipped just inside of his boxers. It was hard to ignore the package underneath that was pistol hard against the thin fabric.

His six-pack didn't disappoint either, a brand resting on the right side of his chest. She knew it was a college thing, lowkey glad he didn't have a tattoo of some chick's name.

Her eyes betrayed her, traveling up and stopping as they met his. He smirked watching her reach for a large, hot pink body pillow that she planned to use to separate them once he laid down.

"I need to shake this monster," he said, looking down at himself then back up at her.

"The bathroom's that way," she quickly said, turning the TV up.

"I thought we were going to lie down and go to sleep," he said, grinning before he walked off. Once he was in there, he left the door open.

He was quiet, too quiet, so Shona leaned over just a little to see what he was doing. His head was leaned back with his eyes closed before releasing. In his hand was the prettiest, thickest muscle. It was curved, hanging about six inches soft where his fingers on one hand held on to his shaft.

Her breath quickened, waiting for him to finish relieving himself. She watched his dick twitch just a little before he was done.

"Ahhhh," he sighed, shaking it. He looked over and caught her staring which made him smiled.

She quickly leaned back, pretending she was looking for something on her side of the bed. He washed his hands and came out, fighting everything in him to respect her mind and body, but his dick was being so disrespectful.

He wanted their first time to be different if there were to be one, so he surveyed her room trying to get his mind off the paradise he knew existed between her legs. He could tell it was good, too. Pussy like hers had to be good since he knew she wasn't giving it up. That meant she was saving it. He didn't care what she said. And for him.

Besides, to him, she just looked like she had good pussy.

He smirked as she busied herself, then looked around. It looked like a woman's room, different shades of pink throughout it from her curtains and pillows to the color of paint on her walls. He could tell she like pink and that she was a sneaker head, boxes piled all the way to the top of her walk-in closet.

That turned him on too. Avery fit the image his parents wanted him to have, but Shona was the type of girl he could just be himself and have fun with. He hadn't smoked in years short of his love for a nice cigar, but if he wanted to get lifted after a long day, he knew he could do that too with her.

He mastered over the years being a chameleon, entering and exiting into two different worlds. That was challenging but necessary. Still, he loved the law and fighting for justice, so when he came home, he didn't want to fight. He wanted to fuck and talk shit with a loud mouth ass girl. A pretty one with fuckable lips like Shona.

"You gone turn that shit off so I can get some sleep?" he asked, testing her gangster now. He was tired of fighting, watching her play like he wasn't even there.

"If it's bothering you, you can go across the hall to Kaleela's room or home. It's your choice," she said nonchalantly, finally laying back as she flipped the TV channels.

"What if I choose to put your pussy in my mouth?" he said, already making up his mind he couldn't leave without getting a taste of her. She caught him staring at her legs, pulling her shirt down.

"Pull it down all you want to, precious. Up in here looking like a dessert and a nigga hungry as fuck."

"Ugh, you're so nasty," she shot back, her face turning red as she forced herself not to smile. X had her leaking and he knew it too.

He walked around the bed and stood in front of her. She squirmed, her breathing picking up as he stood there and watched her. His eyes hung low like he was high and he was. He was high off of her. He thought about her many of days, deciding to leave her alone until he took care of his problem. And one that was compounded as he thought about that fucking box in his trunk.

"What, boy? Why are you staring at me?"

"I stopped being a boy a long time ago," he told her, gripping his dick. "You see that, but if I was keeping it real, that's just one way of proving I'm not a boy. Now my dad," he said, getting serious out of nowhere. "He's the boy. I realized that when I was thirteen. I woke up with my nutsack tight and my Fruit of the Loom briefs wet. Scared the shit out of me. My mama acted like she ain't seen my dick all her life and I thought I was dying."

Shona didn't know where this story was going, but she knew he his mood shifted, so she shifted with him as he seemed to share something deep about himself that maybe many didn't know. He watched her face relax which was a sign she was listening.

She's going be my bitch, he thought to himself, wanting to tell her everything, but scared to run her off.

"My uncle Pokey," he said and laughed softly to himself. "That nigga is crazy. He's married to one of my hood ass aunties. My mama called him up and he came over like his ass was on fire with condoms and magazines full of naked women. As soon as he had me flip through a few of those pages, my joint was up and that same feeling I had that morning was back.

Uncle Pokey brought a cucumber with him, talking about he could tell I was gone be dangerous. Like a champ, he snatched that wrapper off that condom with his teeth, then slowly rolled it down that big ass cucumber. He then handed me one and told me to go in the bathroom.

I can't lie, it felt weird as hell. It was a lil' slippery, but after a few tries, I got it on. Once I came out, he didn't look but asked me if it was on tight with no air at the top like the cucumber."

He paused, deep in thought before he spoke again. "That day I knew I had to be better than my father. He had all this clout in the community, but was never there for his fucking son. I became a man and he wasn't even there to help me navigate through that shit."

By then Shona had turned the TV down. With her arm underneath her head, she stared at him, leaning her head to the side. He cleared his throat, coming out of his thoughts. He felt a little uncomfortable, unsure why he felt comfortable sharing that, but now it was out.

He decided not to overthink it and she helped when she said, "I can relate."

She laughed a nervous laugh, then her face resumed to a serious state. She was thinking how she knew nothing about being a woman and still didn't, but she wasn't ready to share just yet.

When he didn't see her face plastered with judgment, he wanted her more now than ever. Grabbing her by one foot, his pushed her leg out, then the other.

She gasped, but said nothing more as she looked down, avoiding eye contact. He watched her abdomen area contract as she breathed in and out slowly. Taking her silence as consent, X continued to cross the line.

"I can tell you stingy with the pussy, but I like that," he said with a serious look on his face before he dragged her down to the edge of the bed.

She held on tightly to the comforter as he lifted he kneeled down, lifting one thigh onto his shoulder.

"Mmmm," he moaned, smelling a soft lavender smell from her skin that was soft to the touch. He kissed the back of her calf, then worked his way up, stopping right before her center.

She lifted her head just enough, her mouth agape, waiting. Their eyes met intensifying the stillness of the room against her now rapid heartbeat. He smiled, excited it was beating for him. Slipping the thin fabric aside, he planted his lips softly against her center but didn't taste her.

"So wet," he whispered, watching it run down her ass now. "I know this for me."

She said nothing, breathing heavily. She was so anxious for him to taste of her this time as the kiss on her pussy lips sealed the deal. She sat up just a little, getting impatient. He smiled and asked again, "Oh yeah, this is definitely for me."

Her vagina screamed yes, agreeing with him but her mouth had nothing to offer. Stroking his dick, X looked at her wet, sugary lips, imaging just how good it would taste and feel on his tongue.

"Precious, if—" he whispered.

"Yes," she grunted, interrupting him. "It's for you. Please," she groaned, dropping her legs even wider.

He went in, slowly sucking and kissing that pussy that greedily thumped against his tongue, coating it as he consumed her.

"Mmmmm," he said, kissing it once more before he pushed her thighs all the way back.

Her essence showering his face made his dick hurt, craving her even more. He couldn't take it anymore.

"Fuck it," he said, standing up and squatting as he stuck the tip in. She yelped, as he dipped in, then back out, opening her up. He did this over and over until her walls received him.

"I'ma call you Miss Good Pussy," he growled, watching her wet him up. "This tight pussy good as fuck. Yes," he hissed, feeling her pussy clamp down on him. He threw his head back, biting his lip. If was as if he died and woke up in pussy heaven.

"X," she whimpered, feeling him all in her stomach.

"Hm?" he moaned, pulling out and kissing her pussy. He then lifted her up and slid his tongue in her lower hole. Shona's legs shook, unable to comprehend what was going on.

"Wh—what are you—you doing to me?" she cried out as the pad of this thumb worked her center.

Not answering her, he smiled while he tongue fucked her ass so good, she was dancing and squirming all over his face. She heard him laugh as he popped her ass, the sting driving her wild. She begged him to let up but he couldn't, feeling larger than life as he controlled her entire body.

She belonged to him right then and didn't even know it. She cooed and he felt his member jump at the sound of her voice, threatening to spill. It was then he knew he was in trouble. She had mind fucked him too, putting a spell on his dick.

"Shona?" he groaned, closing his mouth and lips over her hole as he slowly stroked himself.

"Yes?" she barely got out.

"When I stick this dick back in, that's it. Whatever you and that nigga had, cancel it," he told her, standing back up as he took his time and eased back in.

He did his research that night after meeting them at the graduation. Chico was friendly yet uncomfortable. Any man uncomfortable in the presence of a woman and his bitch at the same time was a telltale sign they had history.

X wasn't intimidated but he knew a man like him had to have a powerful hold on her, especially since she was still single and this man was very much married to a beautiful bitch with three kids and one on the way.

"O—okay," she managed to say, her voice strained.

Her body then shook violently as he stretched her wide, thrusting inside of her forcefully. He felt everything from the slickness that coated his dick to her heart, beating against the head of his joint.

Her pussy was magical and he was the magician, committing all kinds of tricks to make it come for him. The more she jerked, the faster he went, unable to hold out anymore as she cried out his name in his ear.

"Oh shit, X baby!"

"Argh! Fuck," he grunted, spraying her walls with his seed.

Shona's eyes popped open while his eyes rolled to the back of his head. She then came once more as he continued to pump in her center, planting more of his seeds.

X finally collapsed on her body, his dick still resting inside of her. He couldn't believe what had just happened. Not only had she given him the pussy, but she'd claimed his soul.

He exhaled, feeling their hearts rapidly beating against each other. He couldn't see her, but he could tell she was starting to regret what happened as her body went stiff.

When she tried to move from underneath him, he stopped her. "Naw, not yet," he told her. He rolled over, still inside of her as he wrapped his arm around her body.

Shona was embarrassed, dropping her head on his chest. "X," she whined, feeling him move inside of her. "We can't."

"But we are," he said with such intensity in his voice, gripping her ass as he picked up the pace. "Plus, this pussy not saying no. So fuck it," he told her, grinning. "Sit up." She shook her head no, still hiding her face.

He sat up with her and kissed her on the temple. "Don't overthink it," he whispered. "I'm tired of thinking," he said lowly, rubbing her back.

She felt his words. It was as if he could read her mind. She responded by fucking him back. "Mmmm," she moaned, riding the wave as she rose up, feeling his dick almost in her chest.

He held her tightly, leaning down as he took one nipple in his mouth.

"Ahhhh," was all he heard as she arched her back while his mouth made love to her perfect breast, going back and forth in between the two. "Ugh, X, baby. "

"Yes, that's it. Just next time—" he told her, his voice vibrating against her ear, "—call me daddy. Told you I'm not a boy, Shona. You taking all of this grown man dick," he said, filling her up one last time as he held her against his chest.

"Daddy," she said huskily, smiling.

"Oh, shit," he laughed, then kissed her hard as he held her face with both hands.

X took that declaration as a yes, feeling her fall apart all over him. For the rest of the night, he took his time learning every inch of her body.

"X?" she called out quietly to him, drawing circles on his circles from the accumulated sweat.

"Yes, precious?" She smiled when he said that, but still had to know.

"I thought I was a super star?" she whispered against his chest closing her eyes.

"Damn right you are," he laughed, rubbing her on her back. There was no place he wanted to be except with her. He knew he was in fucking trouble now. "Got to be, girl. Now rest up. You drained all my super powers, crazy ass girl."

Outside, however, a wounded and jaded Avery sat across the street. She had been there all night unable to move. She even held her bladder, releasing all over herself. Most of her threats were just words, but now she knew he meant it when he said it was over.

She'd peeped them that night outside of the strip club. She'd been following the two of them for weeks. She knew X's type. He loved the hood and from the way he stared at her that night, she knew that would be the bitch she needed to take down.

Picking up her cell, she made a call.

"Yeah? Wh—what time is it?"

"It's time to get paid. Tonight, meet me at our spot."

The caller knew that meant they were going forward. It had been months with nothing, but when you owed someone, you waited around waiting for the other foot to fall.

"What time?"

"What the fuck does it matter? Just be ready when I call you back. I need to make one more call. You are on my payroll now," she yelled, disconnecting the call. "And stop calling me got damn London, Tyson."

To be Continued

ABOUT THE AUTHOR

Tisha Andrews a community activist, mother and author hailing from Miami, Florida where she obtained her Bachelor's degree in Criminal Justice and Master's in Social Work. Tisha is also a member of Delta Sigma Theta, Sorority, Inc., an organization that prides itself in social service and the mother of one daughter.

With her combined love for helping others and being an avid reader, Tisha threw her hat in the literary ring publishing her first Novel. Real Love Is Not For Sale in April 2016. Since then, she has completed thirteen novels and is now an independent author, enjoying her self-publishing journey

Tisha also enjoys engaging others, so like her Facebook Like Page, Author "Lil Drew" Andrews, Twitter or Instagram.

What Tisha wants others to know is that none of this would be possible without God. It is her desire to do it all so that he may get the glory. So please be sure to leave a review.